MW01287258

# LUCKY
# TOMORROW

# LUCKY TOMORROW

Stories

## DEBORAH JIANG-STEIN

UNIVERSITY OF MINNESOTA PRESS
MINNEAPOLIS   LONDON

This collection of stories is a work of fiction. The names, characters, organizations, events, and incidents portrayed here are products of the author's imagination or used fictitiously. Any resemblance to actual persons, living or dead, events, or localities is entirely coincidental.

Copyright 2025 by Deborah Jiang-Stein

All rights reserved. No part of this publication may be reproduced, stored in a retrieval system, utilized for purposes of training artificial intelligence technologies, or transmitted in any form or by any means, electronic, mechanical, photocopying, recording, or otherwise, without the prior written permission of the publisher.

Published by the University of Minnesota Press
111 Third Avenue South, Suite 290
Minneapolis, MN 55401-2520
http://www.upress.umn.edu

ISBN 978-1-5179-1927-6 (pb)

LC record available at https://lccn.loc.gov/2025002301.

Printed in the United States of America on acid-free paper

The University of Minnesota is an equal-opportunity educator and employer.

32 31 30 29 28 27 26 25     10 9 8 7 6 5 4 3 2 1

*For my daughters,*
*I love you each to the moon and back, always and forever.*

*You are light.*

# Contents

# Author's Note

Who goes unnoticed and who is unseen?

Not meaning a person who *chooses* to be unseen, like the one who slips by unnoticed at the potluck without contributing a dish. Or the person with eleven items in the ten-items-or-less grocery store lane. Or the child who hides when it's bath time.

I mean unseen people who are discarded and pushed aside, and communities who are undermined and ignored. My life's work is speaking inside prisons across the country. Over the past ten years I've been face-to-face with more than forty thousand women, men, and youth who are unseen by the public. I am a witness to people who go unnoticed behind gates, walls, and bars. This work keeps me in close contact with people who are discarded, and face-to-face with people's humanity when they are at their lowest.

My work and writing spring out of my roots and my life as a multiracial woman in the Eurocentric U.S. culture, where I'm too often viewed as "other" and frequently asked "What are you?" I'm always navigating questions of belonging and identity, seeking places that feel like home, similar to the characters in this collection.

Consider people who go unseen because of the discomfort of difference. Whom do we find easier to walk around, or walk by, rather than acknowledge? I often wonder why we dismiss or want to eliminate some people out of existence.

Through my work with people in prison, I've also grown to believe that for each of us the gathering of all the places we've lived is where we are from. All the places make up our being. Belonging and identity are more complex even for those whose ancestry and birthplace appear to be common and linear.

So how do we carry all the places we are from? Nobody is truly of just one place or one family or one community. Western culture, and patriarchal colonialism especially, views most things as either/or. What about intentionally looking outside the binary and considering both/and as well as and/and?

The stories in this collection are anchored and grounded in four distinct places, equally supporting the characters: the Midwest, where I am currently based in my adult life; Seattle, my hometown where I grew up; Tokyo, where I lived for three years, immersed for my first time in a non-Western culture; and the South, where I was born and continue to travel and speak in prisons.

Here, the characters and their voices are individuals we may not usually listen to, people who live with and/and rather than either/or, and are often made to feel "othered." These stories express all I imagine through everyday people who typically go unnoticed—a solo woman eating in Mickey's Diner in St. Paul, a flower shop vendor in Seattle, a beekeeper on Vashon Island outside Seattle, women in prison in the South, a man on a train in Tokyo.

In our trembling world that is big and wide and complex, sometimes all we have is our immersion in a moment, like a note in a chord. *Lucky Tomorrow* is just this—moments expanded where brevity powers the tension and the characters live boldly in the dignity of their experiences, sometimes with soft fierceness.

This collection of stories is like a constellation of tiny stars. They tether together with a gravity that pulls them into common themes where each character orbits their small world in small moments, living out big questions many people grapple with. Do I matter and where do I belong? This collection also casts a light on the intersection of mental health, substance use, isolation, family, and over-incarceration.

Every day we strive for understanding and certainty. The need is strong for safety, for gathering in comfort. The struggle is real, as we all seek a collective community and to be part of the whole. This is the point of connection in these stories.

The characters here are intimately revealed within their unnoticed worlds. Just as they are in the act of becoming who they are, as they carry all the places they're from, we are also placed in our own locations, our own daily stories of becoming.

My hope is that these stories are an invitation to reflect, look deeper, and encourage readers to wonder: How does it feel to be a person whom others don't see?

# Everywhere at Once

All along growing up I knew two things. First, that one day I'd end up at a public market somewhere, and if I had my dream, near the waterfront. Second, that I'd either be a flower or sell flowers.

Part of that came true. My cousin in Minneapolis called one year, "C'mon, get yourself out of Seattle for a while, do you good."

"We have the best summer public market here. Biggest in the country, second to Texas and none other." She offered to set me up that summer at the market because she had a friend who knew a friend who had connections. So I took her up. Be with family, she said, "I'm all you got, after all."

She doesn't know I had a baby when they locked me up in Seattle. She doesn't know that locked-up part either. They discard people like the leafy stems of wild strawberries, their soft leaves crushed from being gripped as a handle for its tender fruit. She also never mentioned how it feels landlocked in the middle of the country. There's water there with all the lakes, but no salt water tides.

Jimi Hendrix's third cousin twice removed got me pregnant in ninth grade, and no one believed me that I had a rock star about to be born. I forgot his name because it was just a thing in the park one night in Seattle when I had been sent off to a "special" high school. You know, one of those standing-up kind of things in the park when you get too high.

I knew as soon as I smoked my first joint when I was eleven that it was for me. Smoking anything—weed, hash, opium—whatever passed around in the park when I hung out there after school. And even though I hated cigarettes, when someone passed me a coolie, a cigarette laced with coke, I'd toke as much as I could until an elbow next to me reminded me to pass it on. But it didn't take me long to figure out I had my own natural high and didn't need anything else.

My parents thought I was just plain old pregnant and ought to terminate, but I knew she was a rock star in me, a female Hendrix. So they didn't leave me any choice but to run away and have my baby on my own. What was I supposed to do?

St. Ann's Home for Unwed Mothers took me in. Then for some violation I don't remember, they transferred me to a "special" hospital in a windowless van with metal grates all across behind the driver, even removed the handles inside the doors. You could see I was full, and I started labor soon as we got there, and they shackled me to a metal bedpost. Seven and a half hours in labor with a corrections officer sitting there the whole time. Where was I going to go? You know, I tried to find comfort, couldn't move, shackles around my leg to detain me. Handcuffed in labor, then they stole the baby from me right as she popped out. She was born on a Sunday morning too. I'll get her back. Justice is my right. Who does that kind of thing on a Sunday?

• • •

If I ever run into her, I'll know for sure she's mine. So I keep my eye out, my ears tuned. Even if she's all grown up, I'll know she's mine. She'll have that voice, that rock star blues voice. A voice like the sun dances from her breath, and our first hug will melt us together.

Soon as she says, "Hi, Mama," I'll know it's her. Every mama knows the sweet sound of her own child. I bet she sings the latest Mary J. Blige and Janelle Monáe, and can even go old school—like Gladys Knight, or Janis Joplin, even Aretha and Chaka Khan.

I could play my harmonica with her. She'll have one green eye and one brown like me, and tall like me, too, with wavy dark-brown hair and same skin that oozes soft creamy caramel. That reminds me, I'm done taking on OPLC—"other people's labels and categories." All the mixes and multis, is it really necessary to crawl into a box? Hapa, Blasian, Cablinasian, Creole, Afro-Asian, Eurasian, Amerasian, Blaxican, Indipino on and on and on, and back in the day the disrespect of calling us half-breed if we're racially ambiguous. For what? To make us feel inferior? I mean especially if a person doesn't know all she is, and anyway it's all back to America is one big a-little-this-some-of-that. Like me, the color of light coffee with cream and more cream and more. See what I mean?

I'll give her a daisy, pin one on her shirt, and tuck another one behind her ear, slip it right into her soft hair.

I tried being a flower once, sprinkled pollen and petals I'd collected from a clump of pansies, my favorite, the purple and yellow ones. I dusted myself all over, pressing pollen in my hair and into my eyebrows.

If I leave the pollen on me long enough, I figure, it'll soak into my pores and hair follicles and then I'll start growing tiny little buds and blossoms of pansies. I even tried covering my eyebrows with petals so that the pollen wouldn't wash away from any sweat dripping down my forehead into my eyebrows. But that didn't work either.

I tried again. Always go for the try again. If you really want something, how will you know if you never try? Operation Turn into a Flower. This time I stayed laid down so that the pollen and petals wouldn't slip off me. I laid flat for three days. I should have done it for seven days. Don't they say it took God seven days to make the world? Not saying I'm a believer and can't say I'm not. The proof, though. Where is it?

I figure a flower needs at least that time of God's seven days to sprout out of me. I lasted three days, couldn't take that lying down day after day. Just four days short of turning into a flower.

I gave up on turning into a flower, and thought, Why not sell them? Anyone can learn how to buy wholesale flowers in quantity and then mark them up for resale. I built a makeshift flower stand with bicycle wheels and bleached-out barn-wood boards I scavenged from a basement I broke into in the alley behind the market. Maybe I'm building the way for other women to be self-starters in business. I could even write a how-to be your own entrepreneur book, and call it *Declare Who You Are*.

If I'm lucky, I'll make some money at it too. I help other people bring flowers into their lives, and if they're lucky, they'd find their own way to be a flower.

FOR A LUCKY TOMORROW BUY A FLOWER TODAY: the sign I painted in big red letters, same as my first sign back in Seattle. Right on the side of my flower cart off Lyndale Avenue under the bridge where I set up soon as I got to Minneapolis.

In the beginning back in Seattle, my flower cart was just a wheelbarrow. Then I got fancy. I painted Felma's Flowers on the side opposite my LUCKY TOMORROW sign. Out there every day even if it's a typical Seattle rain shower.

I was supposed to be a boy—was supposed to be a lot of things, aren't we all? They planned the name Ferry for a son because Mama got pregnant on the ferry, but then I turned out a girl. I like my name even though at first some think it's a lisp. Nope. So who took over the corner across the street from the main entrance to the market? Felma's Flowers.

• • •

Business takes patience, so I waited for a customer, just like when I started in Seattle. That's when I first sketched on cocktail napkins too. I pick them up at coffee shops, stuff a stack of them in my pocket. Just because I sell flowers doesn't mean I get enough of them, so I draw petal shapes, and bouquets, and single stems in a vase, all with color pencils and sometimes watercolor. Have to use my most gentle touch or the napkins tear.

Can't use oil paint either on napkins or I'd try that. Isn't the fancy art in Europe all painted in oil? One day I'll get to Europe, wander around the Royal Gardens or Pond Garden, how all their flowers are lined up in rows with hedges carved into shapes. Fascinating even though not my style. Not the style of nature either. She wants to grow unlined up and unruly.

My favorite is watercolor, how it lives between intention and spontaneity, and the main character is the water even though color gets all the attention and credit. Watercolors and drawing are my friends and company over anything else, even food, even books.

Soon as I made my first flower sale, a single stem of butterscotch broom, I knew I had it in me. I was in business! My sign worked too. About a lucky tomorrow, and for keeping customers. Besides the regulars, new ones stopped by to ask if it's true—about the luck.

"Absolutely!" I said. They bought a flower, too, from my ever-changing arrangement of the day's most colorful blossoms.

Maybe one day I'll frame one of my napkin sketches and sell that too.

Flowers are all that's anchored in this world, though not for long. At least they have roots. And flowers are always a treasure at first. But they're destined to droop. You can trust flowers, even trust they'll disappear. Flowers make it easier to defy the tyranny of fear inside and to melt the sludge of grief, even help me trust myself.

Flowers are what rescue me from the devouring cloudy skies. My favorite wearing flower is a peach and coral poppy. A bush flower I love is scotch broom, the sunny purple yellow it blossoms. Some people says it's a hazardous weed, but even what's unwanted can be beautiful. And my favorite on-the-ground flower is pansy.

I figure a flower is what's constant in this world if nothing else. Well, that and the ocean waves, the way they want to swallow us up, but usually don't. Some say to offer a small bouquet of flowers to the ocean as a way to say "thank you" and show respect.

Another thing. Flowers are everywhere at once. You can hold a flower in your hand and its fragrance is everywhere. Who's to say that fragrance doesn't come alive five miles away? Like spiritual fuel. All at once. Just like people. Here I am right in front of you. But my heart might be in another city, my fondest memory in a different city, and somewhere else, my yearning for where I'll be in the future. Everywhere all at once.

# Stiff Licorice

A woman with a maroon velvet hat pulled over silver-black hair drawn tight into a low bun gives her server a wide smile. She begins to talk in her retired school teacher robust voice, the strongest in this downtown restaurant. "Tomorrow at two o'clock I'll be seventy-eight," the lady says, "and I'm ready!"

Her server offers a sincere "happy birthday."

Two younger women sit on the far side of Mickey's Diner in downtown St. Paul. They pack into the five-booth train car restaurant. Cars and buses hum along West Seventh, slushing through early spring melting snow past the diner door. A block away the regal and flashy Saint Paul Hotel towers over Rice Park. A few children prance around in the park, and a man leans against an oak tree, his guitar on his lap, not playing. A woman with a flower cart holds court at the center of the park, her flowers' fragrance everywhere at once in all directions.

This is the two women's Mother's Day evening since they lost their mothers earlier in the year. They anonymously send dessert to the lone woman. Her lap holds a clear plastic shopping bag with flowers printed on the outside and a mass of red licorice rubber-banded together and a lottery ticket inside.

"I remember little things," she goes on, "like my sister when she first had a lisp in third grade."

Pointing out the two young diners, the server delivers dessert and the woman juts her jaw toward those distant dessert companions in a single nod. She finishes her strawberries and sponge cake in two brisk bites, pulls money from a black-and-white polka-dot plastic coin purse and marches toward the exit door. She hugs her shopping bag to her waist.

Almost to the door, in a last moment the woman detours toward her dessert comrades, liberates two strands of stiff licorice from her plastic bag and yanks from deep in her overcoat an algae-green New Testament. Pocket-size. The woman proudly presents both the Bible and licorice, clamped in one hand as if handing back graded pages of A-plus homework.

Making best use of her former teaching voice, the woman fills the restaurant with references from Revelations. About angels and stars falling from above, about harvest and locusts, that a thick fog will shroud everyone with uncertainty, and more mighty angels.

"Just once can you order a simple BLT and keep the plagues to yourself?" the server says.

"We don't know if we have another day," the woman hollers. She throws high her free arm, hand open to the skies and fingers outstretched except her thumb, which locks a piece of licorice to her palm. Just as she belts out "One thousand years are ending . . ." the woman's younger sister walks in after receiving the familiar call from the restaurant.

They link arm in arm while the server cups a hand to their elbows. He wishes both "Happy Mother's Day" and gently eases them in the exit direction.

Suddenly the two dessert senders rise from their table and begin to mouth the sound of trumpets. One adds something about judgment and the other bellows "Just wait!" from deep in her throat. "You'll see! You just wait!"

They approach the sisters near the door. Silence blankets the now-crowded restaurant as the server whisks these suddenly self-proclaimed evangelists through the door and snaps the lock shut.

Outside, a light mist descends into the soft spring air. Mother's Day is revived for all four women as the sisters invite their fellow crusaders home for tea and a second dessert. The air is charged with anticipation.

# Except for the Sea

Night darkens on Black Beach in Silver Bay, Minnesota, along the state's North Shore of Lake Superior, the largest freshwater lake in the world. It's the only sealike mass of water in Minnesota, and Black Beach is ten miles south of where the Baptism River feeds into Lake Superior in Tettegouche State Park. The black sand from taconite, dumped into the water for years by mining companies, washes ashore with the waves.

Only a young man is there in the early dusk, just arrived from Minneapolis for a midweek writing retreat. The day before he'd spent all afternoon in reverence of the magical marble carving, the Veiled Lady at the Minneapolis Institute of Art. With tricks of light and polish, the artist Raffaelo Monti created the illusion of a veil, of seeing through the stone. The top of the Veiled Lady's head and shoulders are polished smooth to reflect light. Where the veil falls across the face, the marble is less polished. It reflects less light, giving the impression of texture in fabric.

A quick wind picks up on the beach, and the waters smack the sand and then break onto pebbles. The air is full of spray, anointing the beach. Water carries all his boyhood memories where the sea and shoreline stretch on forever, always eating the earth.

He is spellbound by the power and passion of big waters. It started for him as a child on the coastal oceans and seashore where the crash of waves drowned out people's words so that when they speak, it's just mouths moving. Immediately captivated by his first salty whiff of the sea and its beach, that first breath of its air carved itself into his memory.

He is alone. Festering his whole life, he remembers everybody in their flaws. "Why did I rage against my family and mar them with memories? Wounding them with words."

Nothing matters now. He stares into the darkness, furiously blinking and scanning this strip of black sand for a place to land his gaze. There is a crunching sound of someone trudging over shells. A veiled woman rises out of the waters. A glow at her feet, she stands still, shivering for a moment. As if reaching to embrace someone, she presses forward into the darkness with both arms.

The man on the beach swallows hard and shifts, uneasy, squatting on the sand, hoping the woman will not see him or hear his tears. He looks down the quiet miles of sand. There is nothing to cry about. It is dark. Very dark. The air is alive with his past. He tries to ignore words and worries in his head.

The woman from the water approaches, then stumbles and begins to shake water from her veil and hair. She stands and sings softly. The man remains silent and sitting. Behind him, the woman brushes the back of his neck with her long hair. In a series of quick steps, the veiled woman leaps in large circles, dancing around. She returns to the man's side, leans over and strokes hair from his eyes. Her hands fall away.

The man inhales deep gulps of the cool night air. The only sound other than his own breathing, the pulse of open waters. Stillness, silence everywhere. Except for the sealike lake. And sounds of footsteps splashing as the woman returns to the waters. His joints begin to ache. His heart pounds in rhythm with the splashing waves.

Beneath the warm moon he rises to kneel, knees dug deep in the sand. He listens and gazes intently into the waters where the veiled woman melts into the distance, full round waves rolling against her thighs, then waist and shoulders.

Just as water reaches her face, the woman turns. Smiles. The man stands upright in the night air, turns his face to the mountainside behind him, then walks into the waters. Caught between earth and water, he peers over the edge. The silk of water slides over him like a veil. He spreads his arms to a lowering sky, closes his eyes, and waits.

# The Big Wave

Ramón is the world champion of big wave body surfing. It's a sport for gladiators and solo warriors who surrender to the biggest swells in the sea. It's not the surfer who chooses the wave, it's the ocean that chooses the person and gives them the opportunity to ride the wave. It's a gift from Mother Ocean to float, swim, dive, and dunk under and over and toss around with her. Even when the waves grow still, life is all there at the sea, roaring and real, mysterious and lonely.

Waves are his religion. When he can't sleep, he goes to the waves. Sad, go to the waves. Need to solve a problem, go to the waves. Clears the head. You can see forever thousands of miles and years out into the universe where all at once, everything is transparent, nothing veiled. Water, a place of gracious healing, peace, and perfect safety. For silent reflection to discard whatever skips into your brain. We all need that, the silence.

At dawn every day when the sun rises at the ocean and the sky soaks up its light like a swift milk stain, Ramón gives offering to the goddess of the ocean to ask for safe passing. He walks into the waters with a small bouquet of flowers to show respect and say *Thank you*, then he gently lays the bouquet on top of a small whitecap.

At seaside, nothing but the ecstasy of water and how it moves and speaks its own language, and can fling you into infinity. The sea is a reminder that we're not promised another day. By the sea, everything tumbles out in truth. It gives good reasons to feel small in life's landscape, a tiny dot in the great universe of life, small yet not diminished or out of place.

Sometimes it can be a day of carnage, with the waves eighty feet high where Mama Ocean wins the day, like the time she took his board and snapped it in half.

"You just have to be prepared for what the ocean will give you," he tells the paramedic who seals the gash in his thigh where the cragged edge of his severed board carved into him.

Later on, night settles as soft as a bird floating and fluttering downwind, and the sun sinks behind the rim of distant mountains. "Just be prepared," he thinks in that near-dream state at bedtime, when the day drops down like a diving bird and tumbles out of sight into the beyond.

# Aimless, Forgetting

The bright blue of the Seattle sky shrinks and settles into dusk. I endure another night of restlessness. Edgy. Again. It's the feeling of sharp and sliced up inside like a ripe raspberry balanced on the center of a brand-new double-edged razor blade. No matter which way I roll, I know I'll be sliced.

I walk a lot, not just to get places. I'm a pacer, staying on the move every fresh blue day. A restless urge pushes me to keep on the move. If you stay on the move, it can help you forget what you want and remember the rest you need to keep.

Drinking made life easier at first, then didn't help much after a while. I'd been slamming down shots of Jim Beam on a regular basis since puberty, about the same time I first saw one of my brother's aimless adolescent erections.

Roaming last evening in Seattle's railroad yards along Puget Sound as I'd done many nights, I head out to board the red-eye Vashon Island ferry for a joyride. Ever since I emancipated myself at seventeen to live on my own, I've wandered. Estranged from my family, it's been seven years since we last spoke. Tired of feeling the notice of people all over me, tired of making up reasons and stories about my in-between, half-this, part-of-that, some-of-something looks. I was sure then that someone had been using my face in the wrong world.

I used to want another name to get my head into, a new person, a new name to belong to. At the library one day I scoured old telephone books searching to attach to a different name. Another time I ripped through pages of *National Geographic,* hoping for a new country to belong to.

When the Sound Patrol finds me wandering and talking, she says, "Who you talking to? Nobody else here."

I explain. "My daughter is here, might be."

I keep my eyes peeled all day long. She'll be easy to spot. All the luck in the world I know we'll reunite. I hunt for her along Seattle's downtown waterfront, and if I look hard enough I'll find her one day. I have a picture of her in my mind, how she might have my rounded chin and light caramel skin. Or will she be darker like her daddy? The nurse snatched her away the moment she popped out. Gone. They thought I didn't have it in me to be a mother. Who's to say who will be a good mother and who won't? Taking her away shackled my soul.

That's enough to drive anyone over the edge. That's when I started to see what others didn't. It can happen to anyone. Watch out. In the beginning it was snakes. First in the pond at the park with tadpoles and pollywogs, then in a puddle of rain on the sidewalk. I saw snakes everywhere, terrifying fat ones in the water, water muddy with silt. I saw snakes scramble through everything. One time I stirred clear water at the edge of the Sound, clear to the bottom at the shoreline edge. When I squatted down to peer deep below the surface, long serpents swarmed below.

The cop repeats, "Nothing here," and shifts from one foot to the other, then grinds the ball of one foot into the gravel as if to root herself. "Move on out," she orders.

"Ya see," I say to the cop, and turn to head toward the ferry docks. I'm in that maze of matted moss, looking for a soft patch, a place to untangle. No turns. Looking to find a soft patch to land on. Did you ever watch an ant navigate moss? How about an acre of moss? Then you'll get it.

"Don't ya love it?" I tell the cop, walking away. "Isn't that a beautiful sound, the weighted sound of metal as it drags on the tracks? Love that steel on steel sound."

The cop widens her stance and looks funny at me. The star on her jacket glitters. She's got a bag of animal crackers in one hand, a bag of gummy worms in her other hand. Who's on first base here?

"Tightly woven patches," I go on. "Each turn flows into just another turn, harsh and hopeless." I add, "See, I'm in that maze of matted moss, looking for a soft patch. A place to untangle. No turns."

She says these tracks are for trains, not ants, and shoos me on. "Better quiet down," the woman in the blue uniform says and crosses her arms. "Quit shouting at the water, stop bothering people." So I pocketed my world the way other people do with their secrets and demons.

Before I catch the Misty Mover, my favorite ferry to joyride, I grab a flat stone from the pier and skip it across the hollow waveless waters. It hops along so far it disappears over the surface, probably traveling to the other side of the Pacific, all the way to the Philippine Sea.

The ferry foghorn hooted its truth, and I wish I had my own. Truth, not a ferry.

# Devoured

The Setagaya train threads through daybreak, heading east toward Sangen-jaya subway station.

A young girl mounts the train's wooden steps. Excusing her sleepy bumps against others, she leans silent and strong on a handrail, resting before her day's work begins. At night she goes to dance clubs with friends. She wears T-shirts with glitzy graffiti across her chest. She is letting the green side of her hair grow out.

The girl's mother has already walked the train's wooden floorboards this dawn. As she has tread for fifteen years of mornings, like her mother and her mother's mother. They sell cheap sweets in front of Sangen-jaya, along with cigarettes, hard-boiled eggs, and thick white bread slices bagged six to a package. *1000 Dreams in Our Ovens*, the baker's motto spread across the bread bag.

Nothing is said. The girl will spend her life behind the candy stand, just as she is expected to set garbage out on its sunrise schedule, separating burnable and nonburnable. The girl imagines stuffing the candy stand into the bag of burnable refuse.

Bicycles whiz and Armani suits worn by upright men march by, rushing toward the station stairs where the train tunnel devours thousands of people.

Empty windows watch the girl and her mother, panes looking on like the eyes of spring birds in the country scouting for bugs and worms. A cool early-morning breeze blows through the girl's hair and stirs a few stray papers at ankle level. Somewhere, an empty can of milk tea flaps against a curb.

The girl looks up from her labors of sorting and stacking candy and gum packets and takes in her reflection. Dark alert features and a slight frame more suited for work indoors. Her image interrogates her face.

Without warning, rain begins to wash against the facing window, water rolling like waves. Only that pane of glass receives this surf-like downpour. Raindrops as if tears coming out of her eyes. There is silence. The girl sees her reflection wipe away. She no longer exists, other than in a pool of water collecting into a puddle on the sidewalk.

Later, when sunlight presses against the window and steam rises from the thin pool of water, her mother vigorously sweeps away the slight clutter accumulated before their candy stand. Newspaper and a crushed tin can, cigarette butts along with the puddle, dump down into the drain.

# No Regrets

Tokyo is the world's largest city. I live along a small street in a small building in a small flat, Fuji House, M-5 coordinates on the map.

At M-5 I am holding only a few words of Nihongo,[1] most of them variations of saying *excuse me* or *thank you.*

Walking, silent, from my home to the post office, I fork out whatever yen the postal clerk displays on her calculator for me. There I am at M-5, silent in the grocery store, wondering if certain products are for my mouth or my shoes, for sewing or for washing windows.

Wearing colors that appear neon against others' traditionally tailored grays and blues and browns, I stand at M-5, silent at Wakabayashi Station.

Then, riding in the comfortable quiet on Setagaya's two-car green train, swaying back and forth on old wooden slats. Silence. And the concealed stories rising from the silence of other passengers. Along with inferences, maybe judgments, from corners of their mouths and the place where eyebrows meet.

I consider releasing a lively laugh in the hush. Animated. For no reason. In fact, I think of swinging upside down from my ankles in those stirrups suspended from the bars meant for standing passengers to hold. In my dress with my arms flinging wide around peoples' knees.

---

1. Nihongo: Japanese.

Better yet, I think of wearing Mickey Mouse underwear as I dangle. Even better, I detect a dance behind the passengers' introverted eyes. In the pace of petals opening, silent eyes begin to leap, easing into deep pliés and grand jetés.

Just in case I feel inspired tomorrow, I will wear Winnie-the-Pooh.

# The Bottle Duster

At the center of the day just before Sangen-jaya Station on the Hanzōmon train line, a woman with blazing attentive looks darts out of Miyafuji liquor store gripping a feather duster. Miyafuji Liquors, the only commerce open along Setagaya Dori on New Year's Day in Tokyo.

Corrugated metal panels lock in surrounding shoe shops, fish stands, and other liquor stores, all sealed for the quietest day of the year. Beer and coffee vending machines punctuate every square meter of concrete.

Tokyo winter winds bite the air. A hazy sky hovers, and blue-gray fumes move in from nearby Kan-nana Dori, six lanes tiered three high where transportation engineers study one of the world's most polluted streets.

In front of Miyafuji's plate-glass window, perfectly aligned bottles of saké and imported Johnny Walker Red and Jack Daniel's stand alert, neck to neck in four shopping carts and a wooden crate. She makes ready for closing Miyafuji by early evening and springs from cart to cart with her feather duster batting each bottle. While the neighborhood sleeps, the bottles rattle in her vigorous swatting.

She remains reliable, trades honestly, and hunts for bargains, fulfilling what women do to endure.

The bottle duster breathes Setagaya Dori's powdered dirt down deep. A new year calls forth secrets and taps memories of her barrenness. Her parents are dead, she manages her uncle's store, the only descendant, unmarried, and beyond bearing children now.

Hope dies out of the day. The woman sees her desires whisper away with the dust. Next New Year's the woman resolves to keep Miyafuji open all hours, late into the evening.

# Fountain of Redemption

One rush-hour morning in Tokyo, fitting seven to a row in the subway car, my deep-diaphragm breathing carried me to a distant land, soaring through tall countryside grasses.

I am covered with monarch butterflies who transport me to their hibernation in Mexico. We land on a beach south of Zihuatanejo. A small town rises high above beach cliffs. On the corner of the intersection where El Banco de México sits is a small café with five wood tables and a row of orange birds-of-paradise in a window box.

From this café a person can witness the whole world. On a second-floor balcony somewhere a mother, surprised to find the sun has set, calls to her son to come home. In another place people drift down streets, talking, humming, stopping to point or shop or work. Some probe a satchel or briefcase or handbag. A group of schoolchildren dashes out for morning playtime. Another group, girls hand in hand, lines up single file behind their teacher.

Somewhere else, steam rises from a feed mill across the valley. A woman scrubs the entry to her home, then perches on the front step and reads a magazine. Later on, she props herself against the fence surrounding her home and shuts her eyes. Down the way, two women at a corner wave goodbye, begin to part, then rush back to embrace.

Cities are asleep, and their streets dream of solitude. A forty-something man sits on the granite lip of a fountain, tears rolling down his cheeks in silence. He clutches the edge of the fountain with strong hands. Priest's hands that once presided over communions. Hands of comfort for congregations and worshippers in various countries. Also hands that, in private, loved men and women equally.

He fixes his gaze on two younger men, men in suit coats strolling arm in arm, heads tossed back, laughing together. Elsewhere two lovers stretch out in a park and talk in a hushed tone beside the whisper of the stream winding through the park. Opera music floats through the air, arias in Italian.

The gong from a church tower startles them. The man at the fountain tightens his grip. He has been cast from his calling. First, in a long marriage to his high school sweetheart, he was divinely inspired to contentment with other women. Now, for his desires with men, he is banished.

A towering church steeple next to the fountain strikes top of the hour. The man paces around the fountain, walking close to the ground as if the frame of the sky frightens him. Waters in the fountain gurgle, begin to sputter and spray from the spouts.

These sounds stir me suddenly to gulp for air, forcing my shoulders and back to abruptly expand. To stay small in the subway, I breathe from the top of my lungs. Quick brief pumps of air. On long train rides, craving air, I wish for the bottom of my diaphragm. For long deep inhales. Silent, satisfying. Then my back and shoulders gently force into neighbors on both sides. I feel them move slightly from the pressure.

A push into the man on my right, middle aged, damp as if water has splashed on him. He is dressed with a collar of the clergy, a fierceness in his eyes. I notice his hands clench themselves, fingers that wrap and wring with irregular rhythms, agitated twisting.

Peering back into the train window after I step out, I mourn for the man who sits in a slump, as if a spongy strange melon saved from the trash.

Shortly after arriving home, I take a luxuriously long splash in the nearby pond. As the day breaks away, light pauses on the edge of the urban horizon stretching on and on and sullen below the sky. With a deep intake of the warm night air, my chest rises at the astonishing gracefulness of it all.

Later, I remove a brown mango from the trash and place it in the kitchen window box overlooking the small water fountain in my flower garden. I wonder if fruit were able to ripen in reverse, would it return to its tree?

# French Opera, Chocolate, and Statues

A boy from the Philippines with his mother and brother is on an airplane from Manila, with a layover in Narita Airport in Tokyo, to join their father in Detroit, where Tagalog and opera are infrequent.

When the boy finds out the American lady in the window seat next to him is a minister, he asks where are her statues and the long white dresses she wears. He is five. This is the first time he and his mother have flown. She is leading her children to their father after a four-year separation.

Their father works in a friend's family business and has acquired a title after his name, a company man finally able to buy the house he wants in the right area for his family. A long driveway threads up to his big remodeled house. Three imported cars nest in the garages.

It is early morning, winter dawn unfolding behind the man's house. The air fills with the smell of early snow. A golden glow from the sun makes the ice sparkle. A siren wails in the distance. On a closer look, the neighborhood is broken.

A woman in one house carefully pulls her tea set from its home in a china cabinet. She does this every afternoon in the event a guest might stop in for a visit. Her English linens and Rosenthal have not yet been used.

A man in another house fills his soul with top-of-the-line electronics and a fifty-inch twin picture surround sound television.

Slick TV ads of ski trips, ranch vacations, and safari adventures seduce him. He travels twice a year with a married woman. He has met his dream, retirement at fifty. The man lives alone.

Long slats of light sweep into the airplane window, pierce through thin clouds and cross shadows on the boy's face. He sits wearing airline headsets for the first time. French opera is piped in. Arias and time pass. His eyes appear drunk with the magic and mystery of the music.

After a while his fingers tap on his lap. Only when the first act is over does he reach for the chocolate his mother gave him at boarding time.

A year preceding this trip, his ears every day overheard bits of his grandmother's boasting, a small and strong woman, not yet old. The boy can't find his grandmother in her loose dresses, often layered with a shawl and apron. The boy sees his father the way his grandmother tells it: *can you believe it, by his third year in business . . . a trip to Europe every spring . . . last I heard, snorkeling in the Caribbean.*

The children and their parents finally reunite and renew with tears and delight and reticence. The boys are weary from discovering their father and Detroit all in one day.

Other than a table and four chairs, and beds upstairs, the house is not yet furnished. While the mother coaxes her children to bed, the father sits alone at the dining table. He remembers a time before he was married, a dining table in another house where he sat alone, as he had done for years in a row, at a table set for two. At one time he sat across from his father, who was unable to say *I love you.* He searched through his boyhood for some moment of closeness and recalled evenings when his father said his own father was unable to say he loved him.

The man hears one of his boys upstairs sigh into dream and sleep.

The house, empty as it is—how can there be so many shadows? No one there, his family asleep, a hand touches the man's shoulder. The silence of his father weighs on him like fury itself. His life is going to change. He can feel it.

# I Figure a Flower

My LUCKY TOMORROW sign works magic. I've got my regulars, and then new ones who stop by to wonder if it's true. About a lucky tomorrow. They buy a flower, too, from my ever-changing arrangement of the season's most delicate colorful blossoms.

Sometimes people walk by like they don't see me. Or look right toward me, but just beyond. Like I'm not even there. The ones who do stop, they always ask me what's on my mind. Some people really care. Even some with that C-suite look. I tell everyone the truth. That's what I really sell. First flowers, then the truth. One of the nurses at the halfway house used to say, *Even if truth is cumbersome, raw truth is even harder to cook and serve.* Can't tell if she's one of us or not.

I liked her though. Didn't march all her letters of degrees and licenses and pedigrees behind her name. She snuck in buttered noodles when she could, knew it was my favorite. Even gave me a pet goldfish in a big clear soup bowl for my bedside table after I told her I'd always wanted one when I was a little girl. A sign in her office read *Tolerance Love Understanding Patience.* She wasn't an icy white woman like the ones at the last place. She was from Haiti, her mother owns this facility. Called me Baby Girl, same as I think of my daughter—Baby Girl, the one I lost.

On my off hours I stand in front of the art gallery on the edge of Pioneer Square and park cars for $1.50 each. Same as I sell a flower. Any stem. I let the art gallery parking rates set my flower prices. I figure a flower should cost the same as a car park. Parking those cars, putting things into their places. That helps me make more sense out of life sometimes.

One afternoon the most beautiful voice flowed from the gallery. Like nothing I'd ever heard. Stopped me cold, that music. It was an opera song on the radio. Good thing I wore my fancy jacket that day, the one with a map of the world imprinted into the silky lining. Seems like I held my breath for five minutes straight. I swear it was Aretha Franklin though. Nothing I understood, she kept saying *Nessun Dorma* over and over. Not many lyrics in opera I guess. It was just one song, but it filled and swirled inside me for the rest of the day.

I found the song on my phone. If it had been before cell phones, I would have had to keep it all in my head, imagining every note over and over.

I played it on loop one day at my flower cart. Made everyone who walked by smile. Goes to show opera songs aren't just for fancy people. A top sales day, ran out of flowers.

• • •

I have days where life seems like gargles of static on an AM radio station not quite tuned in. And other days seems like I know just one feeling. Embarrassment. Those times I am so shy I can't even call the operator to get a telephone number.

I don't have to talk too much. It's not that I don't have anything to say. I have lots to say, just can't deposit all my ideas into words sometimes. When the car parking is slow, I stand outside the entrance to the art gallery and recite slices from fairy tales that no one's probably ever heard before. People stop and listen. They smile. Good way to make friends I figure. Not the kind of friends you ever see again. People smile at me, so I know they like me. They probably even love me but don't know it yet.

A crowd favorite is the lost postcard from *Charlotte's Web*. Friendship and courage, who doesn't need that?

*Dear Wilbur . . . .* I stand outside the gallery door, tall and speaking loud and clear like I was onstage. *You left your key at the cottage this weekend. You meant for me to find the key, right? After we napped one last time, before you marched off into the mountains for your vision quest. Only I never slept and instead counted the flutter of your eyelids while I rested my head on the rise and fall of your chest and remembered nothing lasts forever, not even a pet spider in protective custody in Fern's barn.*

*I've left the key under the rain spout in back of the cottage. I'm patient, I'll wait, goodness always comes when least expected around the corner.*

*Love,*

*Charlotte*

My audience of seven stood silent, and I could tell by their wide eyes that my slice of fairy tale made them think hard like I'd read a poem.

*Don't let the crowd dwindle* I told myself. "Ready for the one from *The Velveteen Rabbit*?" I said, and jumped in without waiting for any answer.

"It's the missing journal entry," I told everybody. "Bet no one else knows about this." Just another way I know I'm special.

"Here we go." I pretended to be holding a piece of paper and read from the air.

*Dear Boy, You've ignored me. I've had enough. I got stress disorder from being here plopped along the baseboard in your room where you left me while you played with other toys.*

*If I didn't already have abandonment issues, it didn't help that you never even named me. So I did it myself. My name is Velvet. Mostly because I love the letter "v." Like "v" as in voice. I have a voice! You didn't know that, did you?*

*I'm not waiting for you. Finally today I can walk upright and claim my being, my very being. I don't need you for me to matter in this world. You're not my spiritual ally. I don't know who is yet but one thing I know for sure, some little boy playing with a bunch of other toys and not picking me up with all the hugs and love to share in this world, you're not for me.*

*Did you know that even though I sit all floppy and velvety against the wall, I have feelings? Did you know? So my plans have taken a new turn, which makes your family's change of vacation dates distressing.*

*I was going to wait until you left on summer vacation to fly out of here into freedom. That's another thing you've missed. I can fly. It's not typically a rabbit trait, however, the powers that be have given me this gift of flight. I love being higher. Off this earth. Even if you had picked me up from the floor and placed me high on the shelf, that would've made me happy.*

*Before I go, though, here's the plus side of you leaving me alone:*

- *I'm not covered with your little boy goop and peanut butter fingers*
- *Nobody ever wiped their nose on me*
- *I didn't get drooled on from being a pillow*
- *No one ever used me like a bean bag toss around.*

*Now that I think of it . . . thank you! I'm filled with gratitude that none of that happened.*

*So today I will use my own strength, the wings I've never tried before. Bye, Boy.*

*Yours Truly, Velvet*

"The end," I said. It's my favorite, a man said.

• • •

Seems I could make it a regular thing and sell tickets: *Felma's Fairytale Night.* But between my flower cart and car parking, usually I make enough money to live. But every once in a while business gets slow. Then I round up more part-time work. I started doing beauty makeovers for extra money. You can be quiet then, and I loved working on the body. I use a shiny stainless steel pan for my mirror.

I first learned about makeup when I watched my older cousin in Minneapolis do herself up in the bathroom mirror. Then I studied how they do makeovers in the department store, and the idea of makeovers made me feel I'm doing good in the world. I used some of my flower sales to buy a basic drugstore makeup and manicure kit and started freelance, a stool at my flower cart.

They never let us wear makeup when I was in the House, but at least I could arch my eyebrows high the way I like. Keeps people on their toes, too, my eyebrows of surprise. High eyebrows make it easier to follow through on Number One on my list but more about that later. Helps my eyes look sideways. If you only just look straight ahead all the time, headed north, you're bound to miss at least three-quarters of what's going on around you. There's action behind you all the time, to the sides, too, so look there—south, east, and west. I'd put all that on my list because you need to know it goes with Number One, but there's not enough room on the back of anyone's forehead for all of this, so you better memorize the extra.

"Be a new you," I said when someone planted herself on my stool. Words spilled out of me then. "We are what our cuticles are," I said when a frazzled woman paused in front of me to consider a manicure.

"If your cuticles look good," I said, "then you'll stand right and look good too. That's what people see first, your hands." I made business cards on scraps of flower wrapping paper and kept them tucked in my apron.

# Moment of Truth

When the woman asks, she means well.

Say it's the second Sunday in May, Mother's Day, and say you just landed in Chicago from Minneapolis on a weekend break for the Midwest Bonsai and Flower Show at the Chicago Botanic Garden. You have an aunt you also visit in Chicago this time of year. You do it every year, ever since she moved to Chicago with a man.

But the woman across the hall from your aunt, who's lived there for years, intercepts you when you walk out of Auntie's apartment. Her timing is uncanny. She catches up to your stride as you march out the front door, down the building steps on the way to the train.

—Where you headed? she asks, and you can't avoid the truth because you know that she knows you do this every May when you visit for the bonsai show. You love flowers like you were a master gardener in another life. Bonsai aren't flowers, but you want to learn about their magic, the artful fusion of miniature nature, patience, and creativity.

Auntie says your mama loves flowers, too, but you got nothing to prove it except that one photo, the only one your aunt showed you of the woman other people call your mother. You don't know her enough to call her that. In truth you don't know her at all.

You always want to be with flowers, the beauty, the frail, and the quiet. But this woman, this neighbor, wants more from you.

Every time you visit your aunt, it's the same question from the woman across the hall.

—Where you headed? she asks again. Why ask? you wonder. You know she does it to make small talk but still, every time? The same question?

You draw in a deep slow breath.

—Nowhere, you say, just out. Then you give your please-can-you-back-off grin at her.

But she goes on.

—Me too, she says, out.

Uninvited, she walks with you to the Blue Line. You climb onto the platform together and wait. Can't help but feel a pang of envy for the trains. Their lives must be so straightforward, following that fixed track without any nosy neighbors asking prying questions.

Say you're not one to be rude, so you let her walk next to you. Don't ask, you think. Can we just stay away from the niceties for a change?

—Need help? the woman asks. Her eyes dart down at your foot in a cast.

—What happened?

No, niceties are not nice. Not for you.

• • •

What happened was you broke your foot when you kicked the baseboard out of fury, the rage you can't help when it rises unannounced this time of year. Mother's Day, when little girls doodle on napkins and cards and give them to their mothers in exchange for kisses followed by long hugs. As if that were something you would have wanted to do anyway.

—I got in a fight with a wall, you say, and the wall won.

—Oh, the woman says. Then with no pause, How's it going otherwise?

How's what going? you think, Life, you mean? Or my foot? Or do you just mean how's it going on this street right here, now, walking with you?

Going great, you say to yourself, until you got here, lady, and started to talk to me.

—How's your aunt? she asks.

Here it comes, you think, and you know it's in the next question or two. Odds are, you can calculate the exact moment, maybe even count the words between *How's your aunt?* and the question she really wants to ask. She's always curious. About your aunt, your mother, about you.

Does she know, you wonder, how your aunt has secret affairs with women? Did she overhear the way you did one time? You wish you never knew this about your aunt, never overheard those women with her when you were little, never glimpsed her long body covered by some woman's arched back. She loves sex with men more. You know because she said that once when you were a teen. She shouldn't have left the door cracked, all her groans and moans, her legs hiked up on some guy's hips. You wish you hadn't been there.

—How is she? the woman asks again.

—She's fine, you say.

—She's like a mother to you, huh, the woman says.

Then she slams you with it. Here goes, you know it's next.

—Speaking of your mother, how is she? the woman asks. She leans in, almost in a whisper:

—Your aunt said she wasn't well.

—Oh, nothing much to worry about, you answer and smile to reassure her. It's not as if she really cares. She asks because you know she knows how the medics hauled your mother away in an ambulance that one time she stayed with your aunt. You lived in Tokyo then, as far away as you could get.

Still, you pretend, and force the corners of your mouth up.

—She's fine, nothing much. Nothing at all.

Then there's the moment of truth, the answer you want to give, the story you need to tell but can't. You started out in the nuthouse when your mother was locked up there, popped out behind a locked steel door in the isolation unit, your mother in shackles and handcuffs because her meds weren't working, guards along with the doctor and nurses at her side. You wonder if your baby-soft brown hair got caught in her handcuffs when she held you for the first time.

When she held you for the first time that was also the last. Or did she hold you at all?

Your aunt held you more, held you since your mother couldn't when she was in the nuthouse.

You love your aunt. She hugs you to bits. She taught you how to stand up and speak up, and how women tend to their own. Yes, she's kind of like your mother. But she's not.

• • •

Your mother draws. She sketches with crayons and colored pencil on cafeteria napkins. Your mother gets the napkins from the mental ward in the hospital where she's spent most of her life. A gallery showed her work once, but you were out of town that time too. No one knew where to find you.

You can't draw, but you like to line things up. Pennies, forks, books on the shelf, your shoes. For the symmetry. It makes life safe, like in the nuthouse, you imagine, everything constant, safe if you're alone there, if the guards leave you be.

You wish you could start over. Stay in the mental ward with your mama. She's not in the mental wing anymore. She's on death row. Or a life sentence, no one's telling you. It never was a hospital the way Auntie said when you were little.

You wish they'd let babies grow up with their mamas no matter what. Maybe then yours wouldn't be on death row now. Maybe if she'd been able to keep you, she wouldn't have gone so wack and sliced up that guard to pieces.

Maybe then you'd find it easier to settle down, have your own family, kids and everything, a home. Not so edgy. But then again, maybe it's not such a good idea if you grow up inside the nuthouse all your little girl days. You wish the two of you could start over. On a beach somewhere. High tide out where coconuts float along the shore. A place where nothing but sand can come between you and your mother. This moment of truth, this story you need to tell isn't quite the answer you give to *How's your mother?*

The woman next to you jingles keys in her jacket pocket and the metal sound jolts you back into the world. Metal on metal, it's cozy to you because it's familiar, keys banging metal bars soothes you.

The story you want to tell slaps you in the face. You step back, your gasp drowned by the click click of the train's metal wheels on the track.

—Well, wish your mama Happy Mother's Day for me, the woman says.

People mean well, but you can't wait to reach the bonsai show, to stand still in their presence and pretend you, too, are an ornamental piece of miniature nature. Or pretend you're a flower.

Light shines from the darkness as the train comes closer. You can't wait to reach your flowers, to pet their petals. Even if like everything else they wither, tender blossoms cast to the ground.

# Destined for Fame

It's three o'clock, and a horn blast pierces the compound reminding the women of Alderson they are in prison. They race to their cottages for 3 p.m. inmate count. For Anne Harper, the horn means her afternoon work is over. With rhythmic rectangular patterns, she swabs marble floors in the administration building, vigorously bending and reaching and twisting from her trim waist. Anne mops mostly around the Control Center where foot traffic is constant and concentrated.

Federal workers drop metal tokens with their names stamped, flipping and sliding these IDs onto a metal cradle embedded in a steel ledge framed by bulletproof glass. All encasing the control room where guards monitor moments of freedom, inspecting tokens in exchange for badges, keys, memos, radios, and authority.

In and out, waiting, telling quick insider jokes, more waiting . . . guards, administrators, supervisors, and assistant supervisors sign in and out while Anne swabs with a string mop like a sailor wearing photo identification and rubber gloves and a hair net. It was a strange dance—they with their keys and badges, she with her mop.

"I'm destined to write a novel or movie script one day," she tells the others. "Gonna sell my life story for lots of money." She buys an excessively expensive mail-order script-writing course. A detailed pencil sketch, drawn with the precision of an etching, opens and closes every chapter of her first novel. "Felma in the other wing is the real artist though," Anne says. "She does color pencil sketches on beverage napkins and saves them all, stuffed into a small shoe box."

One evening in the inmate lounge, the first three chapters of Anne's manuscript vanish while she runs on a bathroom break.

Swabbing floors back at the Control Center the next morning, Anne begins again on page 1. Rhythmic swipes of the mop help her find the poetry inside. After punching out from each day's work, Anne writes at night while sprawled on her upper bunk in a dimly lit cell. Every page carries her a breath closer to freedom and maybe fame.

# Fingers

Like most of the women, Anne Harper racks up a list in her mind about unjust events.

Nothin' better to do. The list for her begins on Mondays and Fridays, when she gets searched after returning from morning work release.

All four steel doors slam and echo in series behind her. With no sight of parole, there's no fooling about that sound. First on Anne's list is being locked up far from the roar of the ocean, leaving her to only imagine flowing tides. Waters she's never heard other than from behind bars, waters she'd never seen being that she comes from deep in the hills of West Virginia.

Three days a week Anne goes to work at Montgomery Ward's nursery, stuffing all her gardening gloves into the same crinkled plastic shopping bag and heading for the Dell Street bus.

Most of her gloves are the brown cotton work type, the kind that shed bits of linty fuzz on the inside, especially with sweaty fingers and hands. A few pairs have those little raised green rubber dots for a better grip.

The guard dumps out Anne's plastic shopping bag full of soiled gloves. The guard methodically slips her hand into every glove, guides her fingers into every finger hole, inspecting each one, fishing about for drugs. Little crusts of dirt sprinkle onto the search desk. Anne likes that. Creating an inconvenience.

While sweeping off her desk with the meaty side of her hand, the guard attempts small talk. Inspecting Anne's purse, she chatters on about the nursery and planting season, about the weather and all the different pairs of gloves. ChapStick and lipsticks opened, mascara prodded, address book flipped through, the contraband lighter flicked. Everything becomes a vessel for drugs.

The guard searches Anne and explores places in her purse that are beyond imagination as ideas for smuggling.

Anne and her cellmate explore each other even more than the guard probes. They lie close in their narrow cots used for overcrowding, heat from their mouths wake the other, early sometimes, before 7 a.m. inmate count.

Anne glides her hands and fingers over Charlotte, taking her to the waters where new moons begin. Their tenderness rolls in like waves at high tide, bringing a safety they cannot find anywhere else inside.

One morning music floats through a crack in their wall. The night-duty guard's sturdy voice trickles in from Aurora's cell next door. Aurora, the self-proclaimed in-house prison preacher, a glorious worker of the heavens.

The ladies watch the guard embrace Aurora. Rubbing her deliberately with no apprehension, from hip to shoulder, back and forth, hip to knee and up again, knee to thigh to calf. Aurora lays stiffly at first, eyelids glued closed as if locking in dreams, preserving the enchanted gardens and humid tropics inside.

Aurora calls out God's name almost with the same throaty beckon she tosses from the pulpit, but this, it's not the voice Aurora gives the ladies during her Sunday sermon preaching.

Anne and Charlotte pretend they see and hear nothing. Divinity stays with Aurora.

Outside, rain falls and the world begins to shine and shimmer and shift in its moistness while the ladies rearrange themselves and drift back in time.

Next Tuesday is Charlotte's out date, a plain good day for freedom. It won't be long 'til Anne gets a new cellmate. Someone else who will understand captive tensions. Someone else to ride the high tides.

# Esther Levin, Undefeated

## Yesterday

**Sunday, October 2, 9:00 p.m.**

If it weren't so dark now, I'd go outside. Been trying to get out for a long time. One day it'll be easier but right now, it's not in me.

"Gotta face the fear," I tell myself, "try." But then, no. You don't conquer a fear, you ride it like a current. Working my whole life to lift the tyranny of fear and trust myself.

I have no proof but I got my certainty. One day I'll walk out of here, free of it all. I can take the rain, the cold, even the rare bullet hailstorm that nails Seattle in the winter. But nighttime isn't for me. I stay awake in the dark sometimes and watch the evening through my narrow slot window, watch all night, then sleep in the daytime. I've got the other four windows here in my one-room apartment taped with duct tape. All waterproof and airtight so the dark can't leak in, can't sneak in like a thief and rob my peace.

I live in the short end of the L-shape, third floor, on the top story of this hundred-unit apartment building. It's the oldest part of the building, but there's an upside to everything. Means our wing is next for a round of improvements, maybe a new coat of paint. This must be the oldest building on earth, the way it needs to be updated. And even though I don't have any reason to go out, they could at least fix my door. It's stuck.

It's easy to find me. On the outside of my door, right below the oversized peephole, I duct-taped an arrow that points to my waist-level mail slot. Then above that, "Esther Levin" in big block letters. Duct tape gives my name a silver sheen that reminds the world, "Hi, it's me, and don't forget I'm in here."

Toby across the hall is a smart one. Always says, Stay ready so you don't have to get ready. But for what? That's the thing, not much to get ready for in here other than the mail. She slides mine in for me. Does me the favor twice a week. Maybe someday I'll do something for her one day. I could help feed her kitten. What I'd love is a basket of kittens. We all need something to care about, to care for, to love.

### Sunday, October 2, 10:45 p.m.

Do I ever need some new clothes. Who wants to wear the same thing every day? What about new pajamas? Silky ones. Then I'd squat at the base of my only window, a five-by-two-foot horizontal slot window, feeling sexy in silk, press myself into the ledge and rock until I come under the full blood moon in the night sky. From here I can witness the world, a wide wedge of devil pie.

Last night, just after midnight, I plopped under my window and couldn't even think about that, with the new neon sign on the rooftop across the alley casting its glow right into my eyes through Seattle's usual overcast sky. Damn sign keeps me from more than a good come—my only freedom. I can't do much gazing at the heavens with the buzzing neon from the L-wing of the building. West Seattle Psychiatric Hospital. It outshines the stars oozing from the sky.

On a clear night, the glare of the high-intensity sign mirrors its letters on my wall, the dancing reflection even one more reason to stay awake.

The upside is, at least I'm not in that place.

In my twenty-eight years living in this building, a letter burned out only four times. Good thing, because then there'd be black outside my window.

"Keep it out, keep out," I promised myself when I was a girl, and I coated my bedroom walls and ceiling with alternated strips of wax paper and tin foil to keep the light in, and the dark out. Windows, too, I plastered with foil.

Before I was born, my mother stashed cases and cases of foil and other dry foods in her pantry where she hoarded kitchen goods, all to prepare for the 1962 Cuban nuclear missile threat. I have my own crisis—the dark. And sirens. She said that Seattle prepared for racial reckoning riots like other cities around the country, and that the shrill ten-minute air raid sirens pierced until the siren stopped. If it were me, I'd want to stay in that little box of a room down there, all cozy and crammed in.

Here I am now, enough foil and wax paper for two layers on my walls and ceiling. Roll by roll, I snuck out of the commissary to start my own stash under my bed. I taped and tacked until I lined my room with a rustling nest of silver and shiny wax paper. The empty window in my room watches me. We all have things in windows that watch us, panes looking on like the glassy eyes of eagles on the hunt for bunnies in the country.

### Monday, October 3, 10 a.m.

Monday morning, my day for handstands. Right in the middle of my room, I shoot my feet in the air, happy I don't need to prop my heels against the wall for balance. Blood to my head gives me a brand-new view of the world. A great way to start my week.

A flurry of birds outside flapped by my window last Monday morning during my handstand. Funny how I never noticed until then how the loose brick outside cracked at the inside corner roofline of the "L." See what I mean? Upside down makes the world new.

I can't resist the birds outside. My face close to the window, I spy on them and cluck tsa-tsa-tsa until my mouth is dry. They flit around to nest there twig by twig. Good for them. And for me. The birds agree with me. There's no place like home.

It's also a good thing I don't mind staying inside a lot. Every day's a new day to do what I want. Read or write? Sketch and doodle? Except I ran out of napkins last week. The great napkin famine of 2023. Those are my canvasses. Crayons, colored pencils, even just a lead pencil, I cover the soft paper with blossoms, circles or squares, a poem once in a while. That way maybe she'll do the reverse of me. I haven't seen her since she popped out. I wonder how she's doing with her father? I'm just not cut out to be a mother.

But this is no way to live either. What about today? I can pace around my room all day. I do that enough. Think? I do too much of that already too. Sit-ups or stare into space? Watch TV? Best of all, I might just lie on my bed and relax. Every day I wake up and face the next day, with plenty of food, if that's what you call a slice of baloney, two pieces of white bread, and an apple. My twelve-inch TV brings the outside world to me. Someone stole my antenna, so all that's left is a stub. I wrapped a foot-long copper wire around the remains to pull in a few more channels. My top floor is lucky—we get good reception.

Toby spends all her time soaking up soap operas. Sometimes opera flows from her room, too, all those drama songs across the hall. Public television, their series on Planet Earth, that's my favorite, especially the one on oceans that repeats over and over in the night.

No need to watch news because I overhear it all with my ear to the mail slot. Sometimes I flip open my mail slot to listen and catch snatches through my door. All the talk in the hall is politics these days. And politics is what gets the world in a mess. I'm not the mess. It's out there. In here, no messes, just a little nest of aluminum foil and quiet solitude.

Guess a president was out there once, half white. But we're more than just one label. Identity isn't like some math problem, you can't just add up the parts and get the whole picture. It's how we see ourself.

Wish the woman won.

About time a woman got to be president. It'll happen, just you wait. There's been enough testosterone running things. Like here, the Super in my building runs this place as if he were the principal and we're all a bunch of kindergarten kids. He's one in a long line of supers, every one of them with the same uppity attitude.

I'm telling you. Treat a grown woman like me this way! I'm creeping up on forty-seven. I even have a grown daughter out there somewhere, and you better believe I know a thing or two myself.

Last week the Super tells me he wants the duct tape off. "It can peel the paint and ruin the woodwork," he says.

Who cares about woodwork? I said, when I got bigger problems, stuck in here, afraid of the dark. The dark outside, not in.

But I can't tell him that, in case he'll think I'm weird. So I make up something.

"My eyes are extra sensitive," I say, "even when it's night out. And the dark still has a glare that hurts my eyes. So I gotta keep my windows blocked."

He's got that *You're gonna pay for any damage* look in his eyes and narrows them as he says, "Remember what I said."

"I can get a letter from my doctor next time I go," I tell the Super. I know my stare is better, with my one eye green, the other brown, as I narrow my eyes right back at him.

He glares at me like he knows I can't get that letter.

Everything about him gets on my nerves. That's why I keep my door locked with the back of my one chair propped underneath the doorknob. I make sure he can't get in. The weirdo.

The way he treats me, I don't care if I never go out again because I'd have to pass right by his office if I stepped out of my apartment. He sits in his glass office at the end of the hall like he's king of the universe, tilted back in his chair, his feet propped up on the edge of his desk, and chewing gum like it's cud. I want to swipe off that smirk he slathers across his greasy face as he scratches his sweaty balls through his polyester pants.

Speaking of letters . . . Thump. A thump of truth. A letter will never show up in your mailbox. Maybe no one ever wrote one to you. But you need a letter to prove you're a mother. Or that you've got a mother.

The Home only accepts daughters of mothers who once lived there. Adult daughters, even though you hit forty, they still want proof.

Who the hell still needs a letter from her mother? A note from home—

*Dear So-and-So,*

*Please accept this letter as . . . blah blah blah.*

*Signed—Ms. Whatever*

The thump of proof from the tightrope of your past where you're not sure the woman who raised you is really your mother or an aunt or an older sister, but you can't spend a lifetime putting together pieces you'll never find. Some things are better left a mystery. All you need now is that letter.

And you don't have all day to wait for the mail. Life goes on whether the mail shows up or not.

Forgery, out of the question. It never pays to fabricate. The truth thwacks us upside the head no matter what, even if invented. It's easier to catch the first time around. It's whether you want a split head or not, and then even a note from your mother won't help.

# The Chosen One

One late afternoon after heading north from Alabama through Chicago into Minnesota driving her brother Edwin's Honda sedan on Highway 36 from UPS to downtown Minneapolis, Rev Aurora spins out on ice.

She's new to driving in snow, the treachery of slippery roads, hardly any traction, skidding, sliding, the likelihood of getting stuck in snowdrifts or stranded on the side of the road, how snow obscures the white lines so how does anyone know what lane they're in. The locals call these the hidden hazards of winter driving, but nothing hidden about any of these threats.

Rush hour, 3 p.m. traffic, four lanes, and she's second from the left. It's the first heavy snowfall in weeks. Thirty-two degrees with a glaze of ice underneath. She's in high gear. All of a sudden her car skids into a slow spin at 60 mph, spinning right, slow and soft as a whisper. A near miss with the cars in front of her.

A space opened up on each side of her car, front and back too. An island of quiet. Her car missed both the railing on her left and the cinder block wall on the right. *It's a miracle* whips through her head, the kind where you memorize each and every moment. How the cold air feels chilling your cheek through the cracked window. How the sun slants through the windshield.

Her car stalls suddenly. She looks up and inches away from her window, the hood of a Ram 4×4 pickup facing her. Trucks, vans, and every kind of vehicle slide to a full stop all around her.

Aurora starts her car, turns it around and begins driving again. "Do you think the hand of God reached down to hold me?" she asks the bartender that night over drinks at Liquor Lyle's. "It's like I was being pulled along by all the luck in the world."

*Maybe that's why I'm special. Not the kind of* special *they thought when they had me locked up.*

From that day on, Rev Aurora knew for sure she is a chosen one. One good deed leads to another. "Soon I'll pass a miracle on to someone else," she tells the bartender.

"Thought you quit years ago, went into recovery," the bartender says as she slides a shot of Eagle Rare into her palm. Oh, just having this one, Aurora says after slamming down the bourbon. Just one.

# Edwin in the Ring

If it means traveling to Alabama to stand in for her big brother Edwin at his roadside Gospel Tabernacle, Rev Aurora would do it. RADIANT LIFE CHURCH the flashing neon sign blinked. *Wisdom & Truth* right below it.

Across the street another billboard shouted its message: Start early, stay the course. Build wealth slowly. It's better than building it fast then losing it fast. Then building again, then losing again and retiring with nothing.

Aurora had been banned from the Lutheran Church in the Missouri Synod because of how she loved women.

Edwin's the big reason Aurora got into preaching. He taught her how to preach, that a sermon is supposed to do four things:

1. Stretch your mind.
2. Warm your heart.
3 & 4. Challenge you to be and do your best.

"Preaching is spiritual warfare," Edwin taught his big sister. "What do the people need? Paint a picture and bring them along. Give them a place where the Devil can't get a footing to dance."

Like her brother and all the greats, she'd whip her people into an emotional frenzy like a conductor directing the people's emotions, drawing them into dialogue and encouraging them to punctuate her pronouncements with exclamation and emotion.

Edwin was captivated by visions and voices that first called him to be a prizefighter in the ring before he was called to preach and proclaim the good news.

Edwin always believed in victory. With his powerful stance, he released hypnotic confidence. He could aim, slide, slither, and entwine, fire and dance and evade anything with a one-footed skip and a hop. In the ring or at the pulpit, Edwin would encircle and gaze, then pause to predict the following second.

Not long after Edwin's last rise and fall as a boxer, he took to revival preaching full time. He didn't have to bargain in the pulpit the way he did with his rivals in the ring. His best sermons brought white to his knuckles as he gripped the lectern. His sermon was laced with plain and simple philosophy and personal anecdotes. On the platform he freely wove stories from his past into a rambling monologue, relaxed, as most evangelists, before an audience.

Edwin would testify how he once lived his days snarled and cornered in the ropes of the Devil, defending and dodging the punches of evil. His eyes narrowed as he pronounced, "We're gonna have some old-fashioned Devil-chasing, God-healing revival here tonight 'cause our communities need down-to-earth, heaven-touching revivals to call sin by name and mend broken hearts and souls!"

He paced back and forth as he preached. One hand grasped a microphone, the other pointed to heaven or to hell or dabbed his forehead with a folded handkerchief. His face flushed with passion, and his delivery descended on the congregation with more drama than message.

The audience first responded with polite applause and timid amens. Edwin struggled to draw his people into the service, using the red-letter sentences in the Bible as punctuation. He'd remove his jacket, unbutton his vest, and get down to the work of warming up the crowd, selling, singing, swaying, and shuffling. His pace quickened, and his delivery became rhythmic and repetitive.

Sometimes striding back and forth across the platform, microphone cord draped around his neck as he banged a tambourine from hip to hand, Edwin became God's own super-salesman with a tambourine ministry. Offering his people a few hours of relief from despair and doubt and debt and joblessness, he became an advocate of hope, promising to preach the arthritis right out of your joints.

Edwin's chanting unleashed a swarm of amens and "Preach on!" and "Thankyalaawd!" His people started to shriek and twirl and shout their verbal responses, jumping to their feet to applaud, whirl, dance, and sometimes sing to their inner music in a private moment of divine. He had them like a brush fire up in the hills that flares up once in a while and swoops down into the valley but never gets out of control.

"Haaaaaaaaaaay Sin-NER!" he'd belt out, then snapped his fingers. His tone and timing shifted from conversational to dramatic.

"Tonight's my night for a miracle tonight's my night for a miracle tonight's my night for a miracle," over and over Edwin'd testify through the loudspeaker.

His voices and visions endured for years even as old boxing injuries delivered him into frailty and then dementia.

With Edwin as her teacher, Rev Aurora became one of the greatest revivalists of all time. Her high-octane voice and her spiritual power poured through the air. She'd lay down two planks side by side and stack up wooden crates as a lectern and preach to whatever few people would gather. Sometimes bees would swarm.

One hand grasped an imaginary microphone as she paced back and forth across the planks. Her other hand pointed to heaven or to hell, and in between. Then she dabbed her forehead with a folded handkerchief, her face flushed with passion as her delivery descended on her congregation of bees.

Striding back and forth across the platform, she banged an imaginary tambourine from hip to hand, and her tone and timing shifted from conversational to dramatic. She was happy and people left her alone.

# The Last Haircut

When Rev Aurora's former housemate died, it was on a Friday at sundown.

"She was like my fourth mother," she told the hospice nurse with her first burst of grief, "after the lifelong mother who adopted me, who was after the foster mother or two, and all who came after my source mother, the one who was either homeless or in prison all the time, the one who delivered me there during a long stretch when she was pregnant, me in her belly at the time the judge sentenced her before she cradled me in her strong arms in our four-by-six cell where we lived together until child protection services kidnapped me twelve months later."

We never again laid eyes on each other after that.

Two nights before the last week of her housemate's life, Aurora cut her housemate's hair because it'd been long months and many more months of pandemic since her last trim. Her meds caused hair thinning, and she trusted Aurora.

"You're the only one I want to help me try this wig I got, after you cut my hair."

The housemate said she felt like a balloon with air slowly slipping out, and asked if Aurora had bobby pins.

Happens so, Aurora did, the ones from her mother's bobby-pin collection in a little clear rectangular box that she found in her mother's nightstand moments after she died, along with a scrap of paper with her last shopping list—Honey. Muffins. Not honey muffins but two different items, Honey, and Muffins.

"You're the only one I want to cut my hair," the housemate confided.

One of Aurora's daughters got lost driving in from two states over to visit her own dying mother because she's turned off all her devices since she was sure the government was tracking her.

Aurora put a stool in their bathroom, planted her housemate firmly there because she was on this side of frail and stood behind her, combing her soft steel-gray hair. She'd let the blonde-brown coloring grow out like all the other millions around the world.

She wanted a trim, if you call four inches a trim.

"My mother cut my hair when I was a girl," Aurora said as she started to snip and clip, which by the way she'd never before cut an adult's hair, only her two daughters when they were little girls.

"And she'd bring out her piano stool and set me there on the lawn of our Seattle home surrounded by poplar and maple trees then scatter the hair clippings around the trees. *For the birds to add to their nests*, my mother would say."

Her housemate loved the story so much it made her giggle.

Aurora finished the trim, ran her fingers through those soft strands of gray, and told her housemate how beautiful she looked. She'd just turned eighty.

"I hope I die before eighty-one so when people say I died at eighty, it sounds better than when a person dies in the eighties. Which sounds so old, don't you think?" she said.

The night before the first day of the last five days of her life, the housemate opened the cabinet drawer, boxes of plastic wrap and foil lined up in perfect order because that's how she did everything, symmetrical and lined up, even the drawer with cutting knives and scissors and spatulas, each lined up an inch apart.

She pulled out a snack-size zip bag. Her hair clippings, swatches of steel-gray hair, zipped airtight inside the plastic sandwich bag.

She handed Aurora the zip bag. "You better take this so it won't get lost in the shuffle."

"What shuffle?" Aurora asked, "You mean when things get busy with your family or The Big Shuffle?" The housemate pointed up to the ceiling and the sky beyond.

"The Big Shuffle," she said, and they both laughed.

It was just hours before she slipped under her bed covers, never out again, oxygen streaming through a hose into her nose, her face relaxed, eyes foggy and mostly closed, once in a while cracked open into a sliver.

Rev Aurora leaned into the pillow, whispered "Thank you."

The housemate was cremated. On Aurora's fireplace mantel now, inside a gold trim hand-painted red velvet–lined miniature French treasure box, nest the last evidence of her human form, strands of her housemate's steel-gray hair zipped into a sacred plastic snack bag.

Rev Aurora is ready for next spring to scatter those hair strands for the birds to gather while they flurry to collect twigs and leaf scraps, with no orphan ever left behind in a nest.

# Esther Levin, Undefeated

## Tomorrow

**Monday, October 3, 12:39 p.m.**

A hand slips a tray of food through my mail slot. I'd swear Toby used to drop my mail through there every day about this time. Something must've changed. A new Super? Or did Toby move?

A paper bowl of two slices of bologna, a thin slice of white cheese, and two slices of bread appear as I slide the small plastic tray through the slot. Guess I'm supposed to make my own sandwich. Boiled carrots and applesauce plopped into the same paper bowl. Pretty tasty.

"Thanks for lunch!" I call out, loud enough to cast my voice into the hall. No one answers.

I stretch out on my bed, munch a slice of the lunchmeat, and eye the afternoon sun rays as they slant through my window. I've pencil-lined where the rays hit my wall and over the years I've lived here, my markings turned into a semicircle sketch of the passing days and seasons.

Zip, tear, zip, tear. What's that? So early in the morning? The zip tear startles me as I slide into a morning sleep after my night watch. I know the zip rip sound of duct tape anywhere. Is someone out in the hall cutting tape with their teeth? Are they sealing my door? Or are they trying to pry it open with something? Don't they know it's stuck? Even though my doorknob fell off a while ago, if I want, I could still push the door with my shoulder to check the latch once in a while. Just to see if it'd budge. Not that I want it to open. Just to check.

Zip, tear, zip. That's a dirty trick, if it's Toby out there goofing around. Now I wished I'd kept my landline hooked up, paid the bill because then I could call for help. But who'd I call? I don't have anyone to call after all these years.

Now that I think of it, this isn't half bad, getting my food delivered on a tray like this. There's an upside to everything. My door's stuck so hard, or even if it's taped closed now, I don't need my chair under the knob to keep the Super out. Use it for what it's meant—to sit on. Won't always have to squat on the floor all the time to eat.

Right out my window though, the birds tease me with their life of flight, their freedom as they flutter overhead. When I used to go out, I'd take a slice of bread or a chunk of cornbread that I saved from my lunch to feed the chickadees that hover overhead waiting for tidbits. The last few times I went outside, they chirped, irritated I was late. When I clicked tsa-tsa-tsa with my tongue, a flock of them flew right to me on my last outdoor venture. Oh I bet they miss me now. It's been a whole year that I haven't been outside. Least it feels like a year.

### Monday, October 3, 2:59 p.m.

Another tray slides through my mail slot. Hope it's buttered noodles.

"Esther Levin. Meds," a woman's voice calls out. A paper cup full of pills and next to it, a second paper cup with water.

"It's not like I can't get my own water," I yell through the opening. Two eyes watch me from the other side of my door through the slot.

"Down the hatch," the woman says, "the water too." I grab the cup and swirl the tablets in a circle. I almost get dizzy as they spin around the side of the paper cup like a NASCAR race in slow motion.

"Toss it," she repeats, "or you'll lose your outside time."

Who's she kidding, I think. Didn't she read my chart? "I don't go outside!" I yell through the slot.

I once read my chart with my own eyes when the nurse dropped it on the floor. I peeked through the slot in my door and right there, the top page on the clipboard, in bold block letters:

ESTHER LEVIN # 02751
ALIASES: Franklynn; Felma
AGE: 45
RACE: Multiracial
RELIGION: Jewish
PATIENT does not like noise, or the dark. Refuses to go outside.

And then some small print afterward.

First of all, I'm one-quarter Jewish: my grandmother. If they can stick a number by my name, then they can get the right fraction after *Jewish*.

And if you lived squeezed in a box room like this long enough, plunged into bland routine, you'd die inside too. Between that and the meds, it's all I can do to keep my spirits up. So here it is. Tomorrow at sundown starts the Day of Atonement, Yom Kippur, but nobody cares about that, here or out there. I'm the only one who even knows here. So I'm on my own for penance. We're all alone, each of us anyway.

Who's got the holiday spirit when it's not your holiday? Advent, Christmas, Easter everywhere. I've had twenty-eight years off and on in this wing, but when I was out the longest, just before I was sixteen, I loved the lights and window displays that started in October, getting ready for December. But the down side . . . Jesus songs everywhere. Drove me crazy. That's all supposed to be private, who you pray to or what you believe, not blasted over speakers for the world to hear.

We get the same spread for each holiday here, Thanksgiving,

Christmas, and July Fourth. Three slices of turkey loaf, two white bread slices, and a scoop of red Jello. Guess they don't know about the fasting. We never did that anyway, growing up. Doesn't help you get any more forgiveness.

The women here are quieter on holidays, on good behavior, to make sure they get that special meal. No one yells or screams, no one bangs or kicks their walls or door. Just to get that fancy meal on holidays. No one floods out her room. I'm glad for that. When Toby floods her room, our whole floor gets sopped.

### Monday, October 3, 3:27 p.m.

If it's not going to be sexy pajamas, at least I could use a separate bathroom instead of this sink and toilet right here in my one room. At least now I have a decent view of the bathroom from my bed. I know there's gotta be space on the other side of one of my walls to add a separate little bathroom. I don't need much, not asking for luxury living, not even for my own shower. I don't mind sharing when they take me with the others, but a new real white toilet and sink instead of this stainless steel attached unit. That would really flip my trigger.

Don't go thinking I'm here for that kind of trigger. A new toilet would be better than hot buttered toast. I've never pulled the kind of trigger you're thinking about. But it did come to me, right after my fifteenth birthday, how to solve all my problems. That was the longest time I was out—my first fifteen years.

Just happened to also be pregnant then and almost ready to pop. I did get out once, a few years ago, but it was just for a few months, after a stint in the Westside Halfway House. Didn't work out though. But at least I got to try my hand at selling flowers, my childhood dream. A flower cart near the waterfront at Pike Place Market.

If I could make my parents disappear, I schemed when I was fifteen, then life would be much better. I planned to poison them.

For no reason other than I hated having a family. Not them, just the family idea. As parents go, they were good enough, but at the time it was my only way out. It never stuck with me as a girl, the family idea. As to why, it's a complete mystery to me.

So I asked one of the boys I knew in tenth grade, a boy a year older who always gave me pot, to teach me the furnace workings and draw a map of the furnace rig in our utility room at home. I always hung around with older boys in school. I didn't know any girls. They always made me nervous. Funny, since there's all females on my floor now.

The utility room in our house was just big enough to fit the furnace, hot water tank, washer and dryer, and nothing else. It shared a wall with my parents' bedroom. My room lay across the hall, close enough to sneak back and forth to plot the details of my freedom. My sister's room next to mine was almost as big as our parents' room. Double-paned windows and a stereo set up with two huge floor speakers made her corner room a perfect crash pad. Miss Goody Two-Shoes with her oh-so-perfect attitude.

For days I carried my pencil map of the furnace folded up in my jeans pocket, fingering its creased corners, and pulling it out behind the locked bathroom door, debating what night to make my move.

The night I planned the incident, my mother read in her art studio after dinner. She'd converted our spare bedroom for her retreat, and rigged the ceiling with overhead neon lights to shed even better lighting on her easels. Her collection of miniature antique lamps lit two tables in the center of the room. Three easels with paintings in progress surrounded each table. A deep-seated two-person couch nested in a back corner. In front of it, an upside-down milk crate for a coffee table. The night of my plan, she drank tea late into the night in her art studio.

It got so late, I couldn't keep my eyes open any longer. Plotting the ordeal wore me out. Tomorrow night, I told myself as I slumped into my dreams in the middle of the night. Tomorrow night is just as good, I thought, as I held the folded map underneath my pillow and fell asleep.

The next night after my parents and sister went to bed, I snuck into the utility room and laid out my map on the floor in front of the furnace. While I tried to figure out what pipe to rig, the thought struck me: If my parents die, won't I be an orphan and sent to foster care?

So I crumpled my map, along with my dream for liberation. I threw them both away. There's gotta be another way out of here, I thought as I dragged myself back to bed. The same words I repeat now every night before sleep descends. There's got to be a way out of this six-by-eight-foot tin can. Must be some way out of my room here. Feels like I'm on death row.

But loss and death are no stranger to me.

See, thing is, when I followed my plan a year later, the explosion took them all, my parents, sister, even the cat. I sat on the top of the hill behind our house and waited for the police to come get me. I was wrong about the foster care part. In Washington State, there's the death penalty. That or some permanent lockup like in the place they put me in before. Not exactly sure where they have me now but either way, I'll be fine. The way a cat lands on its feet.

If the death penalty, I get to choose—lethal injection or hanging. I've had a lot of time to learn about both. I've been here so long, I've known women who've gone both ways. I don't mean both ways men and women, but I know that too. I mean poisoned or roped. If America exports its violence like this all over the world, we're in trouble.

# Bone

No one's heard from Etta Robinson since her husband, Silky, died. Silky Robinson was the best blues singer in the Ozark Mountains. His last years he became a recluse, even before cancer rotted his tightly packed two-hundred-pound body to death in their one-room log cabin.

At his memorial service, fifty mourners chant and dance like swirling dervishes around his body displayed on an elevated table. Etta leaps and hops in her dancing, covered with flowers and silk scarves and bandannas. She whirls around the room, then tosses herself on Silky's body, smothering him with memories of their forty-nine years.

Weeping, she lifts herself and dances some more. The whole room dances, including the lone man in a three-piece suit who finally joins in.

Etta invites her closest friends to watch the cremation after the service. They decline. She tells them how the body flailed around in the crematory for two hours. She watched it, then asked to keep the bones. She said Silky wanted her to make instruments from his bones. The cremators would only give her the hand and toe bones.

Funeral services were the day after cremation. As mourners enter, Etta hands out photos of Silky, photos inlaid into matchbook covers, along with incense produced from her husband's cremated remains. Everywhere in the chapel, Etta tacks up pictures of Silky and his former band members, pictures made crooked by the dancing and celebration. A decorative urn with his remains nested in between the photos. She surrounded the urn with candles and covered herself with flowers and silk scarves and bandannas, leapt and hopped as she danced. She whirled around the room, and then tossed herself on the table, her torso pressed against the photo.

After the funeral, Etta is convinced she needs new teeth. She is sure the family dentist put her to sleep during that last cleaning and created a frown on her face and then engraved his initials on the roof of her mouth. When she woke up, she told the dentist: Too much sleep juice. It made me feel like I was pickled. Actually over-pickled, the way cucumbers get soggy from soaking in brine too long.

Newly widowed, anything's possible without Silky to protect her. He left her a bunch of money and some land—a square inch of Alaska he purchased from a cereal box top as a small boy.

Etta filed a malpractice suit against her dentist. Now she disputes the ten-thousand-dollar attorney fees for the lawsuit. Wanting to remedy the dental blunder, Etta searches for another dentist to remove her teeth, to remove the memories and the feelings. Most dentists refuse.

Finally one dentist agrees to grind Etta's teeth down, twenty-one teeth, and start capping them. Etta's convinced a new set of teeth will help her forget. The frown and the initials will be there forever.

Etta soon disappeared, marrying the man from the funeral, the one in the three-piece suit. They live in the same woods, both singing and swirling and dancing with scarves and bandannas.

# Welded Zipper

You'd never know Etta spent time with the likes of her fancy family and their friends who served watercress sandwiches on Saturday afternoons. Always accompanied by homemade mayonnaise, the bite-size sandwiches were triangular with the crusts cut off.

She lost her taste for such food. All she claimed from her childhood of summer entitlement was the urge to smile with a gracious nod when she didn't mean it. Happiness for her back then meant boyfriends, clothes, and jewelry, in that order. A girl with her priorities straight. With the boyfriends, she'd get most everything else.

Her first date was in Atlanta that summer before the arrest. It was the first time a boy actually asked her on a date. When Lamar Bates asked her out, she met herself in heaven. Not the way her family talks of heaven. A different heaven, one where a person wants to return.

There'd been so much intermarriage in the boy's family, he could have been his own grandfather. Word was, lightning struck him once, and it welded his zipper.

Their first night out, Lamar takes Etta to a meat-n-three place for dinner—meat with green beans, mashed potatoes, and macaroni. He brags how he always keeps a six-pack of Pabst Blue Ribbon in the fridge to add color.

Lamar wasn't like the lineup of guys she'd messed around with since junior high, the ones she doesn't remember other than a spark of memory about a party, or a park, or back seat of a car. With

Lamar, Etta knew he cared because the first date they only kissed goodnight. It wasn't until the second night they went all the way.

After sleeping with Lamar, Etta didn't get that feeling as if the whole world turned gray and cold, like after the others. Sex with Lamar wasn't odd and awkward. She didn't want sex with anyone else ever again after Lamar. Couldn't stand the idea of another boy touching her, or her touching anyone else.

Afterward, on their second date, they end up smoking cigarettes in a grim motel room lit by too many forty-watt light bulbs where the thin water-stream in the shower is feeble, like ten people spitting on them.

From then on, Etta wasted her life on bad risks.

# Bees and Honey

My Aunt Fran thought if she could sell God, she could sell just about anything.

When she moved back to the Seattle area after working a few years in the South since she quit preaching, her fingernails cracked and her voice inched higher and higher. She worked for an agency as a nurse midwife evangelist and offered private care in birthing, vaccinations, and evangelism.

After a while the agency that hired her discovered she was preaching to the patients, so they let her go. She was banned from nursing practice altogether and had to take the quickest job she could find to make some money. She ended up in a part-time car sales position, but it turned out to be more than she bargained for. Selling cars is nothing like selling God after all.

Wasn't long before she left her job in car sales, too, and tried her hand again as a home nurse, working solo this time, in secret, doing home care for the elderly, the ones living alone. One of her patients, a former beekeeper, favored her. She mostly kept him company, prepared meals ahead of time, and read magazine articles to him.

When he died, he left Fran his small bee ranch on Vashon Island. He also left her a piece of land in Alaska, a square inch he purchased from a cereal box top as a small boy.

She quit nursing altogether and tended to raising bees and honey on the ranch. After she left nursing and evangelism, her low-toned sermon voice raised an octave. She squeaked in a high pitch on occasion, her voice cracking as if she were an adolescent boy.

She settled on the island into her new bee business. It covered an acre of land, with a three-room cottage among trees. She called it her main ranch house. Finally she'd have a chance to unpack the boxes and crates she'd stored in the basement of the one-bedroom house that she rented as soon as she moved back from Atlanta to the Pacific Northwest.

She stationed stacks of beehives out back on the lot, and a guesthouse log cabin and a natural spring sat a quarter mile behind the main house. She didn't know much about beekeeping when she inherited it all, other than what she learned when she watched her patient, the former owner, when he was well enough to walk the ranch and explain some of the setup.

That didn't stop her from suiting up in the saggy bee suit he left behind. The seam threads were snarled, and the Velcro closures had lost their stick. High-top leather work boots and baggy gloves kept the bees from stinging her ankles, feet, and hands. The bees buzzed around the slope behind the ranch and tended themselves, as bees do, even how some people who keep to themselves like that do, self-contained.

• • •

Not Dex Flutter, though. It'd been ten years since they parted ways. One day he shows up while she's making morning rounds on her ranch. Her brand-new mail-order bee suit had just arrived, and she was glad to finally have one that fit. The old one went into storage, just in case. Out back in the middle of her regular morning rounds, she slid each tray for a quick check on the honey progress and to make sure the queen bee was alive.

"That's it, sweet on up," she said to her bees. She bent over to reach the lower bee tray.

"Sweet on up?" a man's voice behind her repeats. "You were right. You said I'd be able to find you. And I did."

Startled out of her solitude, she slammed the bee tray back into the box. The sudden force stirred the bees into a frenzy.

"Dex?" she said, and yanked her headgear off. "You're out?"

Jeans hugged his legs, no fancy suit. His wrists bare. No glitzy watch or bracelet, not after the time he served for embezzling from the Cathedral of Good News. He looked exposed, vulnerable.

"Was it bad?" she asked, and reached to meet his outstretched hands. "Did they treat you okay?" she asked.

She'd read about the goings-on in prisons, the drugs and violence, the sex. She pushed to the side the thought that he'd been the one who cheated his followers, robbed those who believed in him, believed in his message. Then the thought returned. What would he do to the younger, smaller, more innocent men, some boys even, locked up with him for eight years? She pushed that thought aside as far as it could go.

"I drove up here to find you soon as I got out," Dex said. "It was easy. Everyone knows you, about you and your bee business. They say it's booming."

They stood silent for a minute, still facing one another at arm's length, holding hands. She turned away and took in her ranch, the span of land and all the evergreen trees that towered over ten wooden bee structures. Wooden cottages lined most of the area. Miles and miles of rickety log cabins to the side and beyond the bee ranch, a gentle slope in the back that led to steep pine-dotted bluffs. It was all hers. But, she thought, I could use a hand.

• • •

Dex had aged, added at least a hundred pounds to his once two-hundred-pound muscular six-foot frame, and his hair had turned salty pepper. The glow in his eyes, gone.

"I could use some help," she said, but she knew even then he had little to give.

How the tables had turned since they first met. "I really don't know much about beekeeping," she said.

"Me either," Dex said, "but I can learn. Bet we can figure it out." The wood on the bee structures looked weakened from disrepair, some even splintered.

"How hard can honey be," he said. Then chuckled out, "Get it?"

The prison time had got to him. He smacked his hand on his thigh like he used to do to make a point at the podium in his tent ministry.

After she and Dex reunited on Vashon Island, he never lifted a hand to help with the beekeeping. He made it his job to sit on the porch every day and wave at folks driving by on Highway 12 down the center of Vashon. Then at the end of each day he goes inside to tell her what all's happened outside since the day's start.

After a while Fran dove into depression and stayed in more and more. She let her beekeeping go. One day a skunk toppled the hives, and most of the bees flew away, never to return.

Soon after, she chipped her anklebone on the corner of her coffee table doing the skater's waltz on the dining room hardwood floor in her thin black socks, with the rugs and table pushed back, and she had to prop her leg up on the coffee table to help heal the broken bone.

"Even after I warned against dancing in socks," Dex said, "you kept at it. At sixty-six, bones don't mend like they used to," he reminded her.

Now she stays in, and eveningtime she starts to close up. After dinner, even in her ankle cast, she acts like her cottage is an inn. She hangs chairs upside down on the table, fills salt and pepper shakers, aligns the spices, takes inventory on her linen and paper napkins, scrapes oil off the griddle, and scrubs with industrial cleanser around her stove burners every night.

Then she types their meal plan for the next day, labels it Auntie's Menu, and waits for me, their lone diner.

# The List

I store a list in my head. Things so busy at my flower cart, no time for jotting lists on a slip of paper. Five ways how you look for someone you've lost, someone you want to find. I keep my list posted right on the backside of my forehead, up high inside like a billboard. All I have to do is close my eyes and look up, and I can access the list whenever I want.

Why stuff a paper list in my pocket like everyone else does? Those always get lost, or crumpled and ragged on the edges. My list is always nice and fresh. Looking for someone you've lost is way too important for a ripped piece of paper.

Five ways to search for someone you've lost:

- keep your eyes looking sideways
- remember how things smell
- test yourself
- never forget
- just trust

Can't use cap letters, not enough space up there and only have room for five things. Sometimes, even with my eyes open, I look up at my list as a reminder about my purpose. Everyone needs purpose. It's what gives life meaning.

If people look at me funny, with my eyes rolled up like that, who cares. I know I'm gonna meet my baby girl someday.

Right next to my list, I set out a violet-colored pansy in a blue vase, and off to the side, a picture of a boat sailing across the Sound that I drew on a napkin. That's not all that goes on up there on the back of my forehead either. Off to either side my ears feel bound.

Another thing, I dream of ears. Last time I was in the psych wing of the jail, I listened less than ever before. Thought my dreams would stop that way, the sounds and visions. Sometimes I think I'm over the edge with these visions. Other times pretty sure I'm an intuitive antenna, a conduit for direct reception from the universe. It chimes secrets of wisdom into me and pumps truth through me. Sometimes faint, other times strong. I'm not the only one. Most people have this tuned-in sensitivity to get the cosmic signals, but they lose the data.

In one vision, ears stack in a pile, like a tower resting in a corner of my cell where the ears would dissolve, then remake themselves into new fleshy masses. Then my ears would transform into elephant-shaped ears growing out of my hip.

Once I sprouted two stiff leathery ears. Starting at my hipbones, they slid on a track up and down the side of my almost sixfoot body, raced down to my ankles, then zipped straight up to my head. Where ears belong.

In the silence at the top of my head where ears can't hear, sounds rustle through my head. A nurse near my face, her whispery breath interrupts memories that buzz in the back of my head. She reminds me of when I was five, as soft as ears myself. A neighbor woman nibbled my ear tips then. Never biting, she'd chew and coo. A strange and startling flash of laughter in her voice, she whispered words of how she loved me.

All I wanted then was just deep dreamless sleep. But out here I feed my ears letters, and then the alphabet builds stories from those letters inside my head. After my ears assemble their own words, I pack one, sometimes both ears, into a velvet-lined blue suitcase. That's where secrets and stories suffocate. No suitcase tight enough to trap the visions though.

# Might Tip Over

My people are post office workers, a long line of service people who deliver your messages. Some days I don't have anything better to do than ride back and forth on the ferry between Vashon and Seattle. Water around me helps rid the visions I don't want and gives me my best insights where I see what the rest can't.

That's what flowers do too. Soothe the edge. Even before I started Felma's Flower Cart. Thing is, when someone like me gets a bee in her bonnet to do something, we do it no matter what. There's no stopping me once I know what I want. And if you're in my way, look out. I don't mean I'll hurt anyone, not that kind of look out, even if the shrinks at the hospital think I will. I mean look out world because here I come. Before you know it, I bet a large-scale nursery hires me. I'll start at the bottom and work up. I love watering flowers, how you can be quiet and relax and think, so I hope that's entry-level at the big nursery.

Flowers are all I ever wanted from the time I was fourteen and quit school up until the day the police thought I needed that rest in the psychiatric wing of the jail. They called it an evaluation. I call it a rest. Like the rest of them can go to hell. That kind of rest. They've been evaluating me off and on for twenty years. You'd think they'd have their answers by now, you'd think they'd have all they need.

I planned on working at the market soon as I got released, but the Halfway House had other plans for me. They set me up with a job in mail delivery on Vashon Island on the other side of the Sound. Vashon isn't like the city, where houses sit close enough to kiss each other. On the island, it's a long drive between mailboxes. Instead of postal service trucks, mail carriers there use their own cars. The House let me use their extra car, a 1994 two-tone blue Chevy.

When I sorted mail at the post office, I loved the near-silence, nothing but the flip-flap of envelopes as they're sorted, which helped drown out the man next to me who breathed through his mouth because his nose was always stuffed.

Even though words dance in my head, who says I have to shake them out? It's not that I didn't have ideas or anything to say. I have a lot to say, but I just can't deposit all my ideas into words. Plus, once I get some words in my mind and they start to flow downstream into my throat and mouth, by the time they hit my tongue and the back of my teeth, I don't want my words to leak out into the world.

That's when my blues harp talks for me. I play the same harmonica that Jimi Hendrix's third cousin twice removed gave me in high school twenty years ago. A sound truer than any words. A draw on those reeds, it pulls from an instinct deep inside, the way I can make it wail.

Not having to talk much, that's the upside of my mail job. It makes up for my sore right arm and shoulder. Perched in between the driver and passenger side, I spend six hours a day driving stretched out. I steer with my left hand, use my left foot for the pedals, and lean to the right, with my arm like an elastic band out the passenger side window rolled down to slide open those mailboxes and slip in the letters. When it rains one of those unpredictable Seattle rain showers, I blast the heat and my left foot cooked on the gas pedal. My delivery arm gets soaked in the rain and my right side aches, sore and slanted from my waist up from leaning and tipped all the time.

The constant tilt gets to me, that feeling I might tip over. I hate it when I don't feel stable.

# Inventive and Meant to Be

It's not like she set out to live and work in Minneapolis. Felma's cousin said it turns out it was meant to be though. Even though she said the underlying culture doesn't really let people be totally who they are, like the layers of the climate are also the emotional layers of the city.

"Takes a long time to penetrate deeper than the surface," her cousin said. "Still the best place for me right now."

She started out at the public market in Seattle. Brimming with ideas, she developed a successful line of bee pollen products. She imprinted motivational messages inside the wrapping of every product. Not the biblical kind of inspiration, the other kind.

Her cousin had been in line to inherit her great-grandmother's recycled pallet business on her father's side. The great-grandmother started small, scraping around the streets of Seattle and picking up discarded pallets in the alleys. Repaired any if needed, tacked in the loose nails, renewed them, washed them, and sold them to the local freight and shipping industries who wanted to cost save.

Great-grandmother was strong, able to drag around a twenty-pound pallet to her garage storage in the Central District.

Pretty soon she expanded beyond pallets and into selling the nails that tacked the wood together. She was inventive in business. Nails are like all the other little things you can't see that hold something together. Her motto: *Little pieces cobbled together count more than the big thing.*

She scrubbed the rust off the nails, got them all shined up until she had a bucket full of nails, then sold them.

But as things go, great-grandmother willed the business to her daughter and son equally. This would be her cousin's grandmother and grandfather. Not Felma's people.

The son talked his sister into selling her 50 percent ownership to him for a dollar. Also turns out that the business over generations eventually sold for $74 million. Zero money to Felma's cousin or the female lineage down the line. No one said anything. That's how it happens for women sometimes.

Didn't they know the number 4 means death, a cursed number? So be it. May the motherfuckers rot in hell, the cousin said.

# Dreams and High Hopes Wrapped in an Old Trench Coat

Steam rises from a Seattle street on this rainy afternoon in March. A woman in a beige just-below-the-knee coat stands on her front step, looking to the train tracks west of her.

To the east lies an abandoned urban lot. The woman imagines a temple there, where drum sounds might thump at 7 a.m. and 5 p.m. in soothing rhythms. To the east beyond the curved roofs of neighboring houses and apartments, mountains tower over the wet street, but the woman is not looking in any direction. She doesn't see the rooftops or mountains.

People walk in the rainy streets, but the woman doesn't see people. She fixates on a tiny blue mitten lost in the street. She closes her eyes and hears the waters of her childhood, oceans and rivers. She can smell her mother, the sand of their summers, the oil on skin.

Out of one side of her memory a girl skips, running alongside a river through the dampness of crushed weeds. Smeary stains hug her shoes.

Through the quiet, sounds of a rocky river come up with a rolling tenderness. Shadows darken in the nearby mountain chasms on one side of a valley, all framed in cedar branches. The strong mountain with its smell of new leaves seduces the girl.

She starts climbing up the mountain but forgot the mittens, a present from her mother, the girl's very first pair.

Not long after her gift of mittens, her mother's voice began to falter and life acquired a bitter and concentrated intensity. The girl overheard talk about spiritual torments shattering her mother. She was once a woman who seemed to run on high-octane spiritual power, someone who hated television and loved to work hard at whatever engaged her.

Her mother became gravely ill. Mentally deranged. She seemed to go mad with frequent spells of delirium and would call out with the most passionate words. Words the girl did not understand.

The rest of those days with her mother she spent at their ocean cabin off and on joined by her father, or an aunt, uncle, or family friends bringing chirpy talk and tea and fresh flowers.

There was a drab despair in this oceanside scene and under it lay the urgent vitality of life flowing away while her mother was in her last moments of dying from madness. Right after her mother died, the girl cradled memories in the palms of her hands and then wore her mittens from the can't-see in the morning to the can't-see at night for weeks.

On her front step just now, the woman hugs herself, arms crossed, and leans against the side railing. She rests there and slides down until she is squatting. She gazes at the street. It seems to slant in her direction. The tracks and lot and buildings beyond seem to rumble and shift. She shuts her eyes, presses her palms against her ears to steady herself.

After a while the woman thinks to cup her hands to make that humming sound like sea winds howling through a seashell. The woman feels she is no longer dying, that her life is not dripping away with the sand washed to sea with each high tide.

# Esther Levin, Undefeated
## Today

**Monday, October 3, 5:10 p.m.**

I deserve to be here. Or maybe I don't. Feeling two ways all at once. Can't decide yet but plenty of time to figure that out. I tattooed a tear, bright orange so you don't miss it, under the corner of my right eye. It's for my baby girl. Had her just after I was sentenced. She's my one teardrop. Do you like how it's about to drip onto the bridge of my nose? Mine's simple, not like the stream of tears on another woman's cheek here.

Under my left earlobe, I tattooed a third ear. I want everyone to say, Look, she's got three ears, so they'll know I'm listening extra hard all the time. But even if I strain, I can't hear the sway of Gig Harbor waters out there. So I have to imagine its waveless water lapping the shore. Water and its infinity. Its power's in my soul.

Even though the prison is near the water, I can't even glimpse the harbor from my cell. But when they gave me regular yard days, three days a week out there sometimes, the rich scent of salt and fish in the air helped my soul soar over the walls.

But there's nothing to do out there but pace around for a few hours and feed the birds. So now I stay in and the guard gives me the latest quarterly issue of *Ocean Magazine*. I read it cover to cover, then start over again and memorize the photos of coral reefs and underwater discoveries.

Today's a regular yard day for the rest. More like a one-woman fenced dog kennel run. If I went out, when I used to go out, I'd always take a stack of sliced white bread or stale cornbread I saved for the chickadees. A slice of lunchmeat keeps the crows away from the chickadees pecking at my breadcrumbs. I bet the birds are mad they're not getting their bread bits from me now. Bet they're flitting through the yard, scolding the other women because I'm the only one who fed them.

Now the seagulls are back for the winter, hundreds of screeching gulls overhead. They swoop in and chase all the other birds away. Every winter they invade the prison in swarms. They dive-bomb the prison dumps to snatch garbage bits, fight and wrangle, peck and squawk at each other all winter long, then leave on schedule when spring begins. From winter to spring, until they vanish back to the seashores.

### Monday, October 3, 6:23 p.m.

Last Saturday wasn't exactly a Sabbath kind of event. We went on quarterly lockdown. So for the next four weeks we're in twenty-four-hour cell confinement in our tin boxes. Every October we have this same lockdown, which is more about the guards and their overtime pay, getting extra for their Christmas shopping. I've seen it for twenty-eight years. Pretty soon the guard crew will roam and wreck through the cellblock and tear up our cells with their drug-sniffing K-9s, from cellblock to cellblock hunting for contraband. We all stash or toss contraband until the shakedown guards blow through.

It's not that dope is out of control here like some prisons, and where contraband means a hacksaw blade or heroin. It's lightweight here. But two women in a fight? That's no reason for the warden to lock down the whole prison.

But I'm in this box with my slot window and life is pretty good that way. The upside is anything's better than what's happening to Toby. They just came and took her away to the death house for her execution next week. Her time's up.

She's leaving the rest of us back in lockdown, but Toby's so crazy she never knew the difference. She finger-painted her cell yellow—feces and yellow mustard, and when they escorted her off, she was covered in her own shit. Last week she clogged her toilet, flooded her cell again with feces and urine. I'm talking pure poop mixed with piss and toilet paper. Our whole floor turned into a three-inch sewage swamp. Its overflow flooded her cell, then it ran out from under her door and right into my #7 across from her and sopped the rest of our floor too. Makes me puke and then I have my own mess to clean up.

They turned her toilet and sink water off after that last flood. All day her pleading for drinking water, it's unbearable. The guards ignored her begging, the stench, her filthy cell. Makes you wonder who's on first base around here. Toby's been locked in her airtight strip cell like that for days and not one guard cares. The only upside is Crazy Toby is off her rocker so she doesn't know how bad it is.

At the one-week mark before your execution date, the true sign of your numbered days appears at your door. A blue plastic-covered logbook shows up in the metal bin attached to the outside of your door.

The floor guard looks in Toby's cell every fifteen minutes and logs in the book to report whatever she's doing. Sleeping, pacing, smearing her feces, everything's logged. Are they trying to make sure we're still alive so that we won't get there first, to suicide before they kill us?

That blue plastic-covered book is a reminder for everyone. Every time I glance out my door window, I'm reminded of the dozens of women I've seen logged, then marched off to die.

Last night at midnight, the Warden's assistant stopped at Toby's cell to ask her to sign off on the execution method she wanted: lethal injection or hanging. Washington lets us pick. Are we supposed to be happy about that freedom of choice? If you refuse to sign or choose, or can't, like Toby, then they pick for you. Lethal injection.

They always come at midnight with the form.

Today some guards from the Records Department came and took a photograph of Toby. It's the last thing they do before the death chamber. The Department of Corrections needs a headshot for the media after an execution.

I peek out my slot. There she goes as they march her past my door, chained and shackled, naked and alone. They hadn't showered her in days. What a way to go.

### Monday, October 3, 6:25–8:59 p.m.

Toby out her cell door—I'm glad it's not my time up. If it were, if I ever knew ahead, I'd get that list off the backside of my forehead. You know, clean things up before the end. I haven't looked at it in a long time. Did you notice my eyes haven't rolled up to look in quite a while? It seems forever.

If my day were here, no secrets anymore, nothing hidden, not if we're at the end. That goes for you too. Not that I haven't thought about my list. Do you remember the five? Did you ever make your own up there? If you need help, write me. I'm good at helping. I used to think my eyes, each a different color, led me to see what others don't or can't. Not that I've had much chance. After all, I'm twenty-three hours in my tin can and since I've passed on my one-hour kennel run yard time this last year, there's no one to help.

I mean I would be good at helping, might understand what you need on your list just by looking at you. So write me:

Esther Levin
Death Row, Inmate # 02751
Gig Harbor, Washington

I'd love a letter once in a while. Haven't had one in nine months. Birthing time. Maybe someone's been taking all of these past nine months to write me one heck of a great letter. I can't wait!

The last one was from some journalist or author who wanted my story. For what? I thought. To make you look good? Good that you got my story out of me? Who do you think I am? Your story slut? There's the story the news told, then there's the one I know.

Nope, I said, you can't have it, not any piece of me. This's all I got that's private, this here inside my head. No one can get in there. The more I think about it, the system isn't broken. It's working exactly as it was designed—to lock some of us up, take us off the grid.

Now that I think of it, I'm going to wipe that list right off the inside of my forehead. Right now. But don't go thinking I'll be without. I've got a needle here, contraband hidden in the sole of my shoe, and I'll tattoo a new list, this time on the outside of my forehead. I might even take votes. What goes on my new list?

Like I said, no need to hide, no secrets at the end. If there were ever a time to uncover the secrets of yourself, the time is now. Not that I'm there, but I'm ready for the world to know. Soon as my list is up, well, no need to tell you. Everyone will see it.

Did you think of this? When my time comes, the henchman will have to read my list, right there before his eyes on the outside of my forehead. Hope I get a literate one. Good thing my day's not here yet. It's way down the road, I'm sure of it. He'll have time to learn to read.

Now that would burn me! I go to all that effort, prick by prick to ink my list on the front side of my forehead, and here's some bozo that can't read. He's got the power of my last breath in his hands, in his ignorant feeble-minded hands, and I have to watch him stare at my list, right before they blindfold me, hood me for hanging, wrap me for the rope, get it?—if I choose that—and he can't read one single letter on my list. Not one! Maybe that's who I'll help. Teach the henchmen here to read.

All these years have minced my memories about what it's like to be free. From second to minute to hour, day to week, and month to year after year after year, my mind wants to believe that this tin box I live in, my copies of *Ocean Magazine,* and the birds out my window are all that matter. That and my daughter whom I haven't met. Not yet.

An officer's steps outside my door. I leave my station at the slot window. Chickadees are in full swarm today, swooping around in search of breadcrumbs.

Time to pull my food tray I guess, but the notion strikes me. It's late. They already gave us dinner. Is there a new schedule? But why would that change after all these years?

I peek through my door slot. At least the stench from Toby's cell is cleaned up. But no one's out there. No tray, no guard, no one with meds. Nothing.

Nothing except the blue plastic-covered log in the metal bin outside my door.

I'm not defeated though. Hoping hard with all my heart that my sentence will be commuted. Who knows, maybe I'll be carried into mortality with all the joy of ocean water, flowers, music.

I can feel it in my bones. This sentence to all the things in my life, reduced, with a reprieve granted for my freedom. Either way, death and loss are no stranger to me. There's hope in the struggle. A little down now, but I bet one day they'll put me on a postage stamp. Or make a movie about me, I dunno. Toby always said they'll lower the flag half-staff if anything ever happens to me.

Look at me. I'm a wildflower. They're free and they don't wither. Defeat isn't losing. And success isn't all at once. Defeat is a chance to start new. Fresh. That's something I look forward to.

# Dear Baby Girl

What I know for sure ever since they released me from the institution: soon as I find out where my baby girl is, where she lives, I'll send a letter. Start slow, just one letter a week. They never should have taken her away anyway.

Some people say if you forget the past, then it won't haunt you. But we can remember the past however we want. Take what hurts and give it strength. We're all of our past moments packed and pasted together into every cell of our body. In the now or in the past, no one moment is really about just one thing. And when we imagine, things can be any way we want.

I'll sketch and watercolor flowers around the edges of my letters so that she knows how deep my love is. I've had the first letter written for eighteen years, sealed and ready to go. Soon as I know her address. Tears spilled down my cheeks as I wrote the first of many, eighteen years of letters and drawings stored in a shoe box. Letters are like emotional time capsules.

Dear Baby Girl,
You were my lily of the valley, my hope for tomorrow, the future. Then they took you away. I'll explain all that when we meet. I'm sorry I missed so much. We can make up the time, don't you think so too?

I missed so much. The first time you got your period. Your first date. Your high school graduation. I missed that day in sixth grade, when you first needed glasses and had to squint to see the blackboard. I missed when you learned to stand up straight, shoulders back so people think, "Ooooh . . . look how confident she is!" Even when not.

I missed the chance to cool the blaze in your chest from so many years of masked pain.

Like mine. How to tame the restless tiger inside. I missed the chance to see your profile like mine. To make the bends in your hair act right, like mine. How to salve your dry ashy skin. I missed your telling of how you'll tell your story. I missed you asking me questions while I made dinner: Who made the world? Why do ladybugs have dots on their backs? Are there people who live forever and never die?

Then I remind myself: "wishing if-only" doesn't go anywhere. Never did. Never will.

Some people shoot heroin, others overdose on shame, on guilt, on finding that mental balance where the world makes sense so it won't seem like you're on the AM radio station, static in your head all the time. I've had it all, done it all. And I'm still here for you, still can't stop dreaming about you.

I've always wondered who's going to teach you your brilliance. And I sure hope you've learned how to make a way out of no way. That's what we do.

Write back soon, ok?
ox Mama

Then you'll write me back right away soon as you read the last word. In case you don't, every year I write a letter back to myself because I hope it goes like I think, from my Baby Girl to me, tuck it into an envelope, press it closed, then open it again like I just received the letter.

"Dear Mama," she'll write me.

"When they came to liberate me with a swirl into salvation, a family, a family could not redeem me, I only wanted you. Where are you?

Not at first, a family didn't take me, but then I trickled trickled into a permanent home, and drip, drip, all over me, they gave me music lessons, classes in French and private piano, art and the symphony, theater and opera, ballet recitals in a pink tutu.

For now I'm waiting at the wall of the secret of wondering where you are. I'll make war on the world with the songs I'm writing, singing my own lyrics. My music will travel the world and that's how we'll find each other.

Until we meet, you're like a shadow glued to me."

# Number Four

A cabbie swung her meter off, pulled over in front of my flower cart and jumped out.

"This yours?" she asked me, smacking the palm of her hand on my flower stand.

Her bang shivered several loose boards and made my cuckoo flowers sway. I pick my cuckoos from the lawn in the park. Don't sell them, but they're pretty in water. My favorite wildflower, a sweet face like pansies. And their aroma! Remember what I said? It's Number Two behind my forehead. You should have it right up there inside your head also. Smell. Listen too. You gotta keep the primal alive. Animals do, don't they?

I nodded. "Yep, all mine," and I pointed to my stool. "I do beauty makeovers too," I said. "Want one?"

"I've got a little time," she said as she slid onto my stool. "Just visited my mother. She's a piece of work. After that, I need a make-over."

"You're lucky you got each other," I said.

She pulled her shoulder-length hair into a ponytail. "Slow time of day anyway," she added.

I got to work on her, but her talking all the time made her move too much. I dabbed her face with the most caramel color of my foundation to match her skin tone.

"I do massage, too," she said, "beside cabs." Her hands waved and her head bounced as she went on. "My dad's got a mortuary, so that's where I started out. The family business. I got to know the body structure and muscle groups real good," she said, "for massage."

"Sit still a minute," I said, thinking of my mother when she died, hearing her burnt remains slide around in the box before they set it in dirt.

Was that formaldehyde I smelled? I can't decide if I want formaldehyde or embalming or cremation when I go.

"Almost done?" she asked. She made a sudden turn to face me, and my makeup sponge swiped a thin streak into her mahogany hair.

"I quit the mortuary when I took up taxi driving."

"There you go," I said. So far I'd dabbed on foundation, eyeliner, and mascara. All I could think of now was her face as if she were dead and getting beautified for a coffin viewing. She was enough for me to know I couldn't do this much longer. My stomach hurt worse at the thought of dead bodies, hurt more than when I had my baby.

Her talk of embalming and muscles reminded me of those splayed frogs in ninth grade biology, poked into wax, waiting to be slit open. If I hadn't gotten pregnant that year and dropped out of school, slicing up those frogs was enough to make me quit school anyway.

The cabbie looked in the mirror. "Looks good," she said, handed me five dollars and stood up.

She walked away and called out, her back to me, head sideways. "You know, at first I thought you were the girl my father hired to help at the mortuary."

I tossed my makeup kit onto the cart to go after the cabbie. "What'd you say?" I asked as the plastic makeup case clinked and scattered across the sidewalk. "What girl?"

The cabbie turned around as she reached her cab.

"What girl?" I shouted, but she'd already climbed into her car. She rolled her window down. "Some girl, said she'd been without work for a while, that she couldn't find enough gigs in the clubs."

The cabbie cranked the ignition. "The girl was a singer," she said, "acted like she was a rock star." My heart lurched with hope.

She pumped the gas over and over. "Some kind of blues and rock singer," she added. "Sang jazz too. Really good!"

The engine sputtered, then died. "I hate when she keeps flooding."

She turned to me and let her engine sit a second.

"Anyway," the cabbie paused and fluffed hair strands out of her ponytail shape, "I thought you were her, but you're a little older than the girl. Good thing you're not old enough to be her mother. She said her mother was off in some nuthouse."

I wished my ears had zipped closed then, that I could erase the list inside my forehead.

This time, when the cabbie turned her key, the engine revved. "Funny thing is," she said, and shifted out of park, "that girl had one green and one brown eye. Just like you."

She shot her hand out the window and waved as she floored it.

"Wait!" I yelled. "What mortuary?" but she'd already turned the corner.

I spent three hours in the library, easy to do because I love any chance to spend in the library anyway. I scoured the phone book because I don't like the internet, and I wrote down all the mortuaries within five miles of Seattle. All eighteen. Then I headed down past the market so I could sit in the railroad yard to plot my action plan. I'd take as long as I needed to visit every mortuary in town to find her.

I told you, didn't I? Number Four on the list. Never ever ever forget. Not deep down, I mean where the back of your spleen touches the base of your spine. Never forget.

# Always There

After probing around in the library for hours one day, Felma tipped over the edge and found herself committed to another extended stay. Soon as she got out, she heads straight for the railroad tracks below the Pike Place Market downtown near the water where she last left her cart. The bright blue of the Seattle sky settles into sunset, and its last rays cast on the empty tracks. It's her favorite place to roam, the way they lead on forever, a reminder that she's alive, belongs in the world. Her eyes fierce and bright, her mind going a mile a minute.

On the way away from the railroad yard, she passes by a cart. No sign on it, only a bare spot as if there'd once been a sign. Part of the first few letters of the former sign are faded: FLOWE . . .

New shelves in the midst of a remodel are filled with beaded necklaces. A man leans on the cart. Ragged slips of paper with lists written on them poked out of his army coat chest pocket.

"What happened to my flower cart?!" Felma asks. A small crowd browses the bead collection.

The man crinkles his forehead, puzzled.

"Always beads here," a woman said as she hands the man a twenty and stirs her hand in an open box of beads as she waits for change. She takes a handful and they sift through her fingers.

"What's happened?" Felma says out loud, not asking anyone in particular. Her eyes glaze, hypnotized by the beads raining through the woman's fingers.

The flowers. Westside Halfway House, the psych ward. What about the cabbie and her story about the girl? Did any of it happen?

"Didn't there used to be flowers here?" Felma raises her voice so the crowd could hear.

"Didn't there?" she shouts louder.

The man shook his head and ran his jagged fingernails across a row of necklaces to make the beads jingle. "Been here for years."

# Edge of the Pond

My aunt invited me to move into her guesthouse cottage on Vashon Island, a twenty-minute ferry ride out of Seattle. I had just returned from my visit to Minneapolis. She's a cousin to my mother whom I never met, but she's more like an auntie to me. She's the one who was mostly there when Mama was locked up, always in and out.

"Your mama needs to stabilize and regulate herself," my aunt would say, "so she's getting help with that." My aunt, always the hopeful one. I must've got that from her.

I set up in the one-room original tiny log cabin out back on her bee ranch, enough room for a single bed, an armchair, and a farm-size table that took up most of the room. Shelves cut from logs lined the walls where she stored her dusty Bibles, an Old and a New Testament, along with some family pictures and a few figurines. A film of ashes coated the bottom of the stone fireplace in the corner.

My first night there, I slept soundly, then in the middle of the night, a sting to the outside of my left thigh woke me.

I jumped out from between my sheets, landed against the heat register, and slammed into one of its raw metal corners. My landing marked its path. Deep slices and scrapes traveled from my forearm, elbow, to shoulder.

I stretched and yawned out of this mess, then whisked myself up from the floorboards. Wounded and hungry, I got an urge to eat one hundred pieces of toast.

By the time we met for toast the next morning, my oozing wounds started to scab over.

"I'm certain a bee sting zapped me," I told her. "A hive at the foot of my bed."

She said it was strange how a hive formed as I slept.

When she started to laugh to herself, her shoulders shook and her back bounced in silence as she listened to my story. When she started to laugh to herself, I suppressed my own quiet laughter to protect the six-inch shallow incision on my shoulder.

"Satan himself invited these bedroom bees," she said. "Satan, whose appetite is never satisfied."

"So why do I get such a personal welcome?" I asked her.

"We all live right between heaven and hell, but some are just closer to one or the other," she said and shrugged. "Maybe 'cause you're not living as close to your God-given purpose as you should." She left the armchair religion from her past behind, and more and more stepped up onto her invisible soapbox, preaching her own personal concoction of salvation.

Several weeks after, I sat at the edge of the pond in the woods behind my cottage. I leaned at the base of a mossy hill, my feet in the pond. I found an old rusty ash bucket there, the kind used to empty a fireplace. I held it under the stream of water that trickled down one side of the mossy green hill and into the pond.

I propped the pail at the place where the sparkling stream seeped out of the fuzzy moss. When a small goldfish swam into my almost filled bucket, I headed home to set up a fish bowl. I'd always wanted a pet fish. Ever since I was a little girl.

I stomped back through layers of fallen autumn leaves. A fast wind picked up and started to whisk through the woods. I quickened my pace as the air whirled. Leaves flew and smaller branches snapped and bent. Pine needles whipped around like sharp pins. When the wind swirled faster, I covered my face with my free hand, then buried my head into the crook of my elbow.

As I raced out of the woods, more and more water spilled from the bucket. The skies darkened, and the water in the bucket started to swirl and swell up in small waves, churning as if it were a minia-ture ocean. Pretty sure, small whitecaps, too.

Suddenly the wind stops and the flying leaves settle. The wind clears a path ahead through the coat of colors. Orange, yellow, and red leaves whisk away, guiding me out of the windy woods.

My bucket of water settles down too, and I glance inside to make sure there's enough water left for the fish.

In the still quiet water's surface, an image of a woman's face smiles out from behind a narrow shadowy slit window frame. I reach in to touch the woman's face. Her cheek feels familiar, silky and soft. By the time I'm back at my cottage, the image had disap-peared. But I kept that softness a secret, holding it in the palm of my hand.

# Spiritual Torments

For a few weeks now, my aunt has stayed inside the cottage and counts on her live-in companion Dex to catch her up and fill her in on who's driving in what direction, who's headed for the city, who comes back, and when.

Immobilized with her chipped anklebone, with Dex always on the verge of dozing, Fran sits around and reads her not-too-risqué novels. In between four-page chapters she gazes out the back window to see the unworked land where she's sure Seminole graves lie buried.

Did she forget she's in the Pacific Northwest and not in the South, where Seminoles once lived? Is she slipping?

"I heard once to place a chair by their graves with food and water on the seat," she said. "Not to feed the buried, but as the dead's last gesture of hospitality toward passersby." So every once in a while she spies a new mound, sure it's an ancient gravesite, and sets up a chair, food, and water, then later brings it all inside. "I figure everyone's had a chance to eat," she says.

I visit more often these days, but never past dinner hour anymore. These past few months, I brought over just-finished romance paperbacks to help her pass time. I go in the morning, when Dex makes more sense. His latest dance partner was on the edge of dementia and that was clear as soon as he arrived on Vashon. One time I had to stop him from tossing a shoe box filled with slips of paper into the fireplace when he thought it'd make good kindling.

I stopped in the main house one day to drop off some more

books I'd collected for her. Her ankle had healed by then, and she was out back behind the ranch house, puttering with the few bee hives left. When I walked in, Dex patted the couch next to where he sat. Newspapers and magazines covered the coffee table, and below the table three shoeboxes lined up in a row, each bound with a three-inch-wide rubber band. I knew to never touch my aunt's boxes and stacks of papers. She had her own way of organizing.

When I sat by Dex, he just stared out the window as if I weren't there, as if he hadn't invited me to sit by him. Then out of nowhere he asked me, "Does your memory flutter, fly to the surface? Like mine?"

"Not really," I said, "but I've had memories, imaginary I'm sure." Mine was more random discomfort, I thought, not memory, not a flutter.

Then a thought flashed through me, and I wished I had a memory of my mother whom I never met. For a long time after I found out I'd been born in the locked unit of the mental hospital where my mother was under care, I'd had a body memory surface about her there, but nothing I have words for. What if I'd ended up growing up locked up with her?

The only photo I'd seen of my mother was the high school yearbook when she and my father dated. They'd never married.

• • •

"She couldn't shake the Devil out of her," I overheard my aunt say to the neighbor once, and my father only said she had recurring "episodes."

My father took me for a little while right when I was born and that was the last of a mother. We never talked about her. "You're better off not knowing," he always said, and I believed him. Anyway, I always had my aunt.

Dex went on, "My memory has sound, a crackle, sometimes a rumble of indigestion."

After the fear lifted about what it might be like in the mental place, and the fear that I might end up crazy too, that it's hereditary, then something close to the need for revenge set in. Only I didn't know whom to "get." My mother? The mental hospital? My father, for knocking her up? God, for making her crazy in the first place?

I didn't know the target, so just in case, I pretty much thought everyone was to blame. It sat like a moody stew in me, with nowhere to pour out.

"You know," Dex went on, "memory has taste. Bittersweet and shaped, clotting with despair, the congestion of no hope."

"Geez Dex," I said, "think of your sermons when you used to preach. Back in the tent. Try to go there, to think when you had hope. She needs you now, and not to dissolve in despair."

Then he suddenly switched and said, "Or memory is sweet like hay, cropped and bundled for aging."

I looked up and my aunt stood in the doorway, listening. She was limber again and able to walk and stand after her ankle healed.

Across the room in his armchair, Dex started to whistle and cluck at her, the latest in his repertoire of sounds from dementia.

The space behind her eyes held back sorrow at the thought of losing Dex, again. First he went to prison for embezzlement, and now this, a verdict worse than a prison sentence. At least in the mental place or prison, sometime's there's an out date in sight.

●   ●   ●

Evening is now my aunt's favorite time, when she sits by Dex and reads while he dozes. She gives the word *e-ve-ni-ng* four syllables, and each one flows off her tongue with a smooth soft roll. *E-ve-ni-ng*. She still closes up the house at night like a coffee shop. That's when I usually head outside to walk the grounds to escape, since at any moment she could set me to work like a waitress. And no telling when Dex might sit me down for another memory flutter and stop making sense altogether. Though at this point, did he really make any less sense than everything else going on?

Out there on the terrain between the chair snacks and failing beehives, and inside with my aunt's latest furniture rearrangements and setups, Dex stopped his waving at cars from the porch. I figured he didn't have his insights anymore either, about who drove by and where they were going.

After a while, my aunt and her neighbors came inside and ate from the fruit and cheese plate and cookies the neighbors brought.

Soon after, she grew gravely ill. Mentally deranged. Her voice began to falter. Once God's own super-saleswoman with a tambourine ministry, someone who hated television other than the preaching shows, and a woman who loved to work hard at whatever engaged her, my aunt acquired a fierce intensity.

Spiritual torments shattered her. She ended up with a head full of stories that never got told the same way twice.

By the time my aunt reached her edge, she acted half-mad, padding around in two layers of wool socks, even in the summer time, wearing a hand-stitched quilted vest over her wool dress and chattering on, with an aura of intensity, about promising a vow of silence like cloistered nuns in retreat.

During her frequent spells of delirium, she would call out words I could never understand. On occasion I'd catch pieces of her stories. One time she mentioned a brief stint as a chaplain in West Seattle's psychiatric hospital.

"I can't believe you never told me this before!" I pound out at her. "How could you keep that from me?"

As she leaned forward to say more, she turned her face close to mine. Her eyes fill, she cups my face in her hands, and before any words come out, she slumped off into a confusion I couldn't understand.

Just when I started to ask for details, she swam off into another spell of delirium. ". . . hospitals are full of folks who could use more God."

She huffed a bag of wind out of her lungs. "Prisons too," she added, "but what everyone righteously needs is . . ."

Her cheeks puffed out and she exhaled a soft sigh this time, but no more words.

Then she drooped into a sitting-up catnap. By the time she woke up a few minutes later, she forgot what she was saying.

She faded, as did her stories. Her voices and visions endured for decades.

# Ashes to Ashes

One night when the dwindle of the day snuck in and after we had buttered noodles and peas for dinner, my aunt had a sudden turn-around of her mental state. She called me into the living room. We sat side by side on the couch.

"Here," she said, and handed me one of the shoe boxes I'd seen underneath the coffee table.

"I've saved these for you. Ever since you were little. Your father wanted me to keep them for you." She placed her hand on my shoulder.

I braced one of the boxes between my knees and pulled the rubber band aside. Underneath the band, on the box in curly hand-writing: *For Ruby when she's older. For her lucky tomorrows.*

As soon as I pulled the band off, the top released and sprang off from pressure behind it. Paper napkins with colored pencil sketches spilled out.

"Wait," she pressed her hand on top of mine. I looked up to meet her eyes, and they crinkled in worry.

"I meant to show you these sooner," she said, "to tell you." She paused. Nothing followed.

I couldn't wait for her to go on, and I started to sift through the pile. Napkin after napkin, cafeteria size, with a soft blue logo printed on the bottom corner of each: WEST SEATTLE PSYCHIATRIC HOSPITAL, DEDICATED TO LIFE AND LIVING.

Colored pencil drawings covered the white on each napkin, each one different. Scotch broom blossoms on many of the napkins, others just scribbles of abstract streaks and circles, and others concentric squares drawn like a maze, fine lines leading into the center, drawn with control and purpose.

I pushed deeper into the box and landed on a stack of napkins with just words, still written in color pencil, but no drawing: *A flower is a home, but I like to roam.*

On another: *Dark at night, dark inside. Can anyone find me?*

My stomach started to ache, and I leaned back into the couch for a second, still holding the sides of the box with my hands so that it wouldn't spill on the floor. Fran sat speechless at the dining table across the room. I hadn't noticed she'd moved from my side at the couch.

I cupped my fingers under another handful of napkins in the box. Twenty times my name danced across the thin paper of one of the napkins. *Ruby,* written with each letter a different color, in the colors of spring. The *R* in blue, the *u* in green, *b* in yellow, *y* in red, but the colors blurred because the napkin was blue.

One napkin looked almost like a watercolor, of a woman and a little girl at the seashore. Shells scattered on the beach. Blues and a peach-colored sky from the sunset glowed off the paper. My eyes fill a little. I love this, I said out loud, and reached to touch my fingertips to the woman on the napkin. Mama's good, I thought.

• • •

I had to catch my breath, and glanced over at the dining table. My aunt's leaning on her elbows, braced, her forehead pushed into the palms of both hands. Her head still down, she said, "Your mother mailed these to you from the hospital. Month after month after month. Your father and I were afraid to show you so he saved them."

"You knew?" I asked, and wiped my face on my sleeve so that my tears wouldn't drip on the napkins in my lap.

"We promised to wait until you were older," she said.

I didn't have it in me right then to get mad at her. I piled my new treasures into a neat stack and lined up the edges, then placed them back in the first box. When I took the band off the second box, the lid popped off the same way and more napkins sprang loose, but this time a photograph slipped out.

Its corners are tattered. Right in the center, a tall woman stands on a street corner I recognize as the edge of the farmers market on the waterfront. She's wearing a hat pulled down low on her forehead and a raincoat even though it looks like a dry day. The woman is gripping a handful of daisies, their smiling yellow petals high in the air as her arms stretch overhead into a V shape. Her feet are apart and legs firmly locked so that her whole body is shaped into an X. I turned it over and read: *Out and about for my birthday! December 30. Happy New Year!*

I dropped my hands down to my side, and the box tilted off my lap onto the couch.

"You knew?" I turned to Fran. "All this time you knew where she was?"

"Didn't know, Ruby, she just mailed these with no return address, and that's why your father insisted you never get the mail, even when you got old enough."

"You knew!" I banged my hand on the couch and some napkins fluttered to the floor. "All this time whenever I asked, you knew she cared about me!"

Her gaze dropped into her lap. "Actually, your father never even told me about these until he was sick. Right before he died, he gave me the box, before you came back for the funeral. He knew I'd do right by you."

Afterward, back at my cottage, I covered the table with a carpet of my napkins. I found myself waking up night after night to go through my boxes of napkins, my only connection to my mother. I stared out my cottage window day after day, staring at the dry parched land where no rain had fallen for weeks.

In the middle of the night a few months after I inherited my napkins, a fire started out back. A calf that belonged to one of the neighbors wandered into Fran's backyard, and some of the bees that swarmed loose stung it. The calf stampeded and knocked over a candle I'd left burning on the picnic table outside where my aunt and I'd just had a candlelight supper.

All of a sudden the dry grass behind the house became a gathering in flames. The unusual absence of rain that month turned the island's dryness into kindling. There had been small fires on the island already. The day before, several stores in town near the pier burned. That fire left the volunteer fire department exhausted, and they were slow to respond to the emergency call I made.

Even the surface of the water on the pond in the back of the ranch shimmered with the reflection of heat and flames, before the flames died on the water's surface.

A strong, dry wind across Puget Sound made matters even worse, blowing the fire toward the guesthouse cottage where I lived. The fire jumped back behind the house and a burning timber landed on my cottage, and in what seemed like minutes, several fiery tin missiles ignited my cottage. One by one the bee structures burnt while my cottage turned into a smoking ruin, reduced to blazing ash.

The stable collapsed, and a cow ran from the barn, a moaning ball of fire. We ran to the pond in the middle of the ranch. Water, my place of healing, became our refuge as we squatted on the stone pond bottom, in the middle of charred water lilies.

By the time the fire department arrived, it was already too late. The fire swept out of control.

While we waited for the firefighters to smother the flames with water, I buried my face into Fran's chest, and for the first time noticed her flat chest from her mastectomy, with no foam bra fillers.

The air filled with red sparks and cinders and looked like a rage-filled scarlet rain. The roaring crash and collapse of my cottage, burned from top to bottom in minutes, fell behind as the fire department drove us all to safety. An angry heat of fire filled my soul. My one link to my mother, her drawings and the one photograph of her, in the ruins. All eaten by the flames.

We returned the next day after the fire died. A gentle rain in the night left coolness in the air. By daylight, my cottage, nothing but ruins. Other than fallen cinder and ash, Fran's main house remained untouched by the flames, but dry ash layered on the plot of land that once held my cottage.

Shaken and stunned, a throbbing pain washes over me. My shoulder joints began to ache, worsened by the skin on my chest hurting as if to burst and blast my joints out of my body, its physical manifestation of heartbreak. I pressed my hands to my collarbone to hold myself together.

As I dug through the damp ash and charred wood, a thought flashed through me for a moment, the image of my mother at the Market, her smile, her arms high in the air, her hands filled with daisies.

All I ever had of my mother now rested in a pile of white ashes. I bent over, then knelt and dug my fingers into the remains of my mother's napkin sketches. My hands coated with caked ash as my tears dripped into the white dust.

I cupped a handful from my burnt cottage and raised my arms above my head as if to make an offering. Bits of ash stick to my damp cheek, and I pressed it with the palm of my hand, wishing I could seal it into my pores.

A quiet wind picked up and caressed my face. The breeze set the ashes free, a gentle scattering of my story into the world a little at a time.

# Afterword

For context, I'd like to place myself within the themes of these stories. A federal prison in West Virginia is my birthplace. My birth mother was charged with drug-related crimes, and pregnant with me at the time. Rather than receive rehabilitation and support services from the courts, she was sentenced to ten years. At that point I was stolen and transported by a federal marshal across the country to Seattle while she continued her sentence. That was the last time we were together. My next stop was foster care followed by adoption.

So I am from all these places, from each family, from every institution. This uprooted beginning is in part how I came to believe that people are from all the places where we've ever anchored. It's also how I am so keenly aware of who is unseen.

We might not know another's pain. This list identifies just a few of the unseen, and many are people of color.

- individuals experiencing mental health crises
- people with physical disabilities
- elderly people confused or struggling with mobility
- someone asking for money or standing with a sign for help
- people with substance-abuse issues
- religious missionaries, people offering spiritual or psychic services
- tour guides or promoters
- someone handing out free samples

- charity fundraisers
- protesters and demonstrators
- community organizers
- street vendors
- people unhoused
- someone distributing flyers or pamphlets
- artists showcasing their work
- street poets, spoken word artists, street musicians
- animal rights and environmental activists
- political campaigners, volunteers asking for signatures for petitions
- people conducting surveys or market research

Writers who create fiction where social issues are woven into the characters' lives, like the ones in this book, are faced with multiple decisions about words. In these stories, the characters face their own mental health, incarceration, addictions, ethnicity, race, gender, sexuality, religion, and disability. I consider my word choices with care and respect for the characters' struggles and victories, and also for how words might affect readers. I use language as it shows up to me from the characters, and it's impossible to get everything right. I have done my best.

• • •

To my parents who encouraged my curiosity and brought me into a world of books, music, and art, thank you. For my birth mother, my deepest gratitude. Without your legacy and the incredible story you gave me, where would I be?

Thank you, every early beta reader over the past so many years of writing this collection, too many to name, along with friends and everyone else who supported, reviewed, and helped edit these stories in all their variations and versions over two decades. So as not to leave anyone out, please accept this broad sweep of deep gratitude.

Numerous grants supported writing time for this collection so that I could settle into the characters in these stories and listen to their voices, desires, fears, hopes, and needs.

A special thank-you to my editor Erik, and Emma, and Carolyn for introducing us. Thanks also to Paula for such gentle copyediting, plus everyone at the University of Minnesota Press for helping get this book into the world: I appreciate all your efforts.

I can't end this without acknowledging all the women and men behind bars. I believe in you. Keep the hope, keep your spirits up.

**Deborah Jiang-Stein** is a writer, public speaker, collaborator, and author of the memoir *Prison Baby*. She is founder of the unPrison® Project, which works with people in prisons to mentor about life skills, coach about recovery from addictions, and build hope. She received a L'Oréal Woman of Worth award, recognition from the McKnight Foundation, and support from the Minnesota Regional Arts Council and Minnesota State Arts Board. Her interviews and essays have been published in the *New York Times*, *Washington Post*, *Wall Street Journal*, and *People Magazine*, as well as featured on MSNBC, National Public Radio, and CNN.